W9-AHR-859

For Emile, Elsie, and Emma —*M. R.*

With all my love to little Fred and
enormous thanks to Audrey and Daniel —*K. M.*

Text copyright © 2013 by Michael Rosen
Illustrations copyright © 2013 by Katharine McEwen

All rights reserved. No part of this book may be reproduced, transmitted, or stored
in an information retrieval system in any form or by any means, graphic, electronic,
or mechanical, including photocopying, taping, and recording, without prior
written permission from the publisher.

First U.S. edition 2014

Library of Congress Catalog Card Number 2013944084
ISBN 978-0-7636-6438-1

CCP 19 18 17 16 15 14
10 9 8 7 6 5 4 3 2 1

Printed in Shenzhen, Guangdong, China

This book was typeset in Shannon Book, Kosmik, and True Crimes.
The illustrations were done in mixed media and rendered digitally.

Candlewick Press
99 Dover Street
Somerville, Massachusetts 02144

visit us at www.candlewick.com

SEND FOR A SUPERHERO!

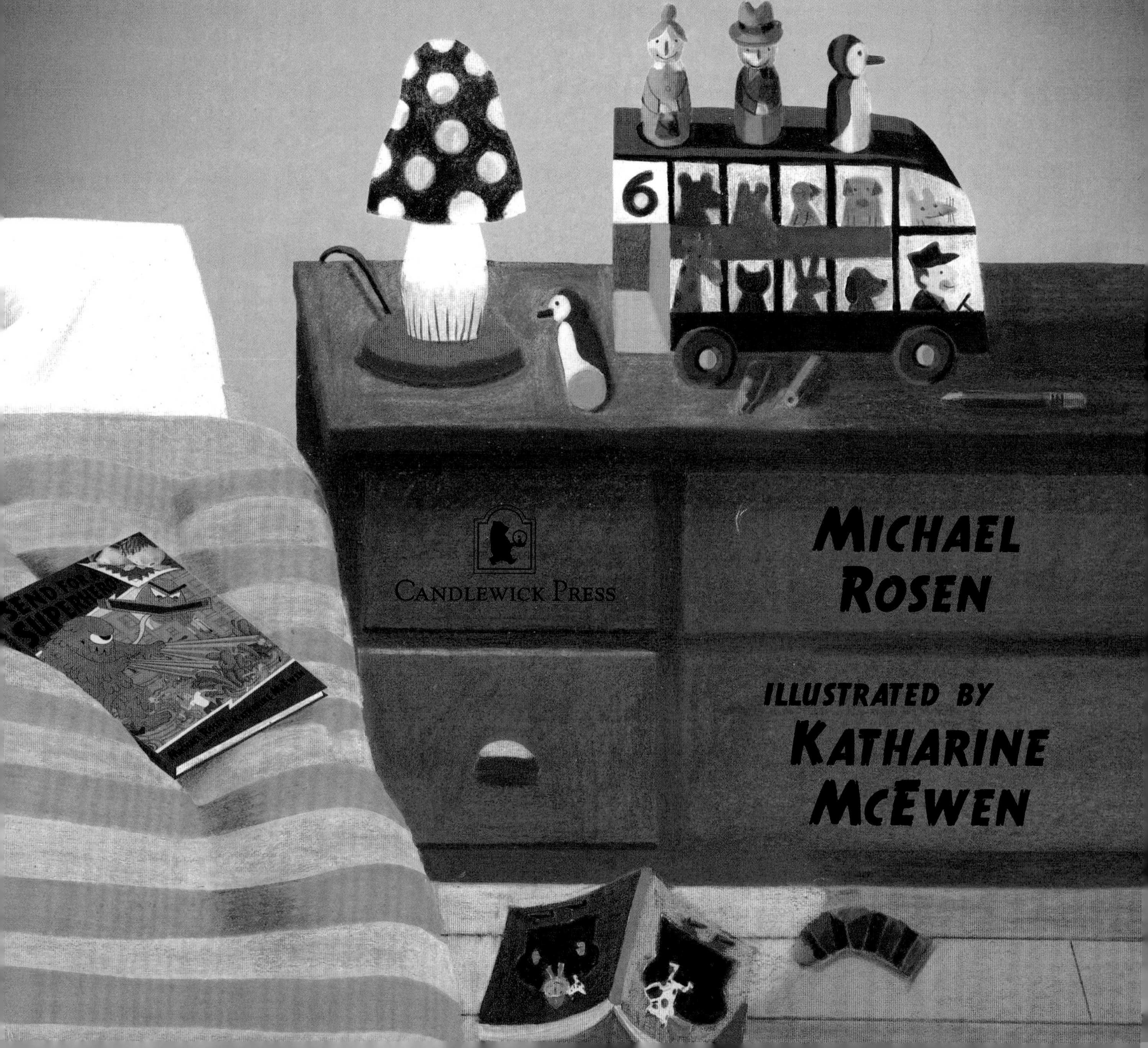

MICHAEL ROSEN

ILLUSTRATED BY
KATHARINE McEWEN

CANDLEWICK PRESS

It was bedtime, and Dad was reading
Emily and little Elmer a story.

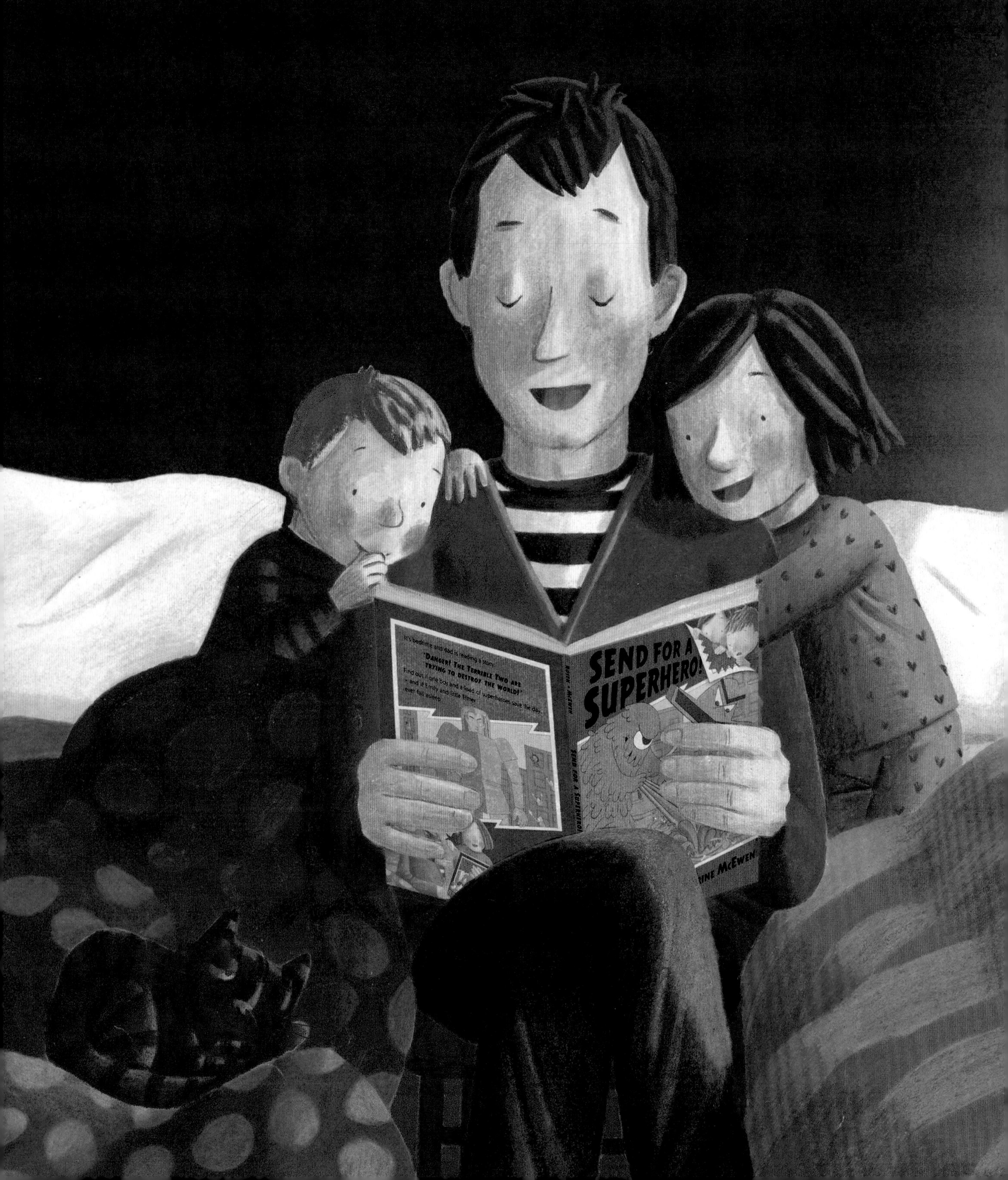
It's bedtime and dad is reading a story!
"Danger! The Terrible Two are trying to destroy the world!"
Find out if one boy and a load of superheroes save the day, – and if Emily and little Elmer ever fall asleep.
Rosen • McEwen
Send for a Superhero!
SEND FOR A SUPERHERO!

"Danger!" Dad began. "The Terrible Two are trying to destroy the world!"

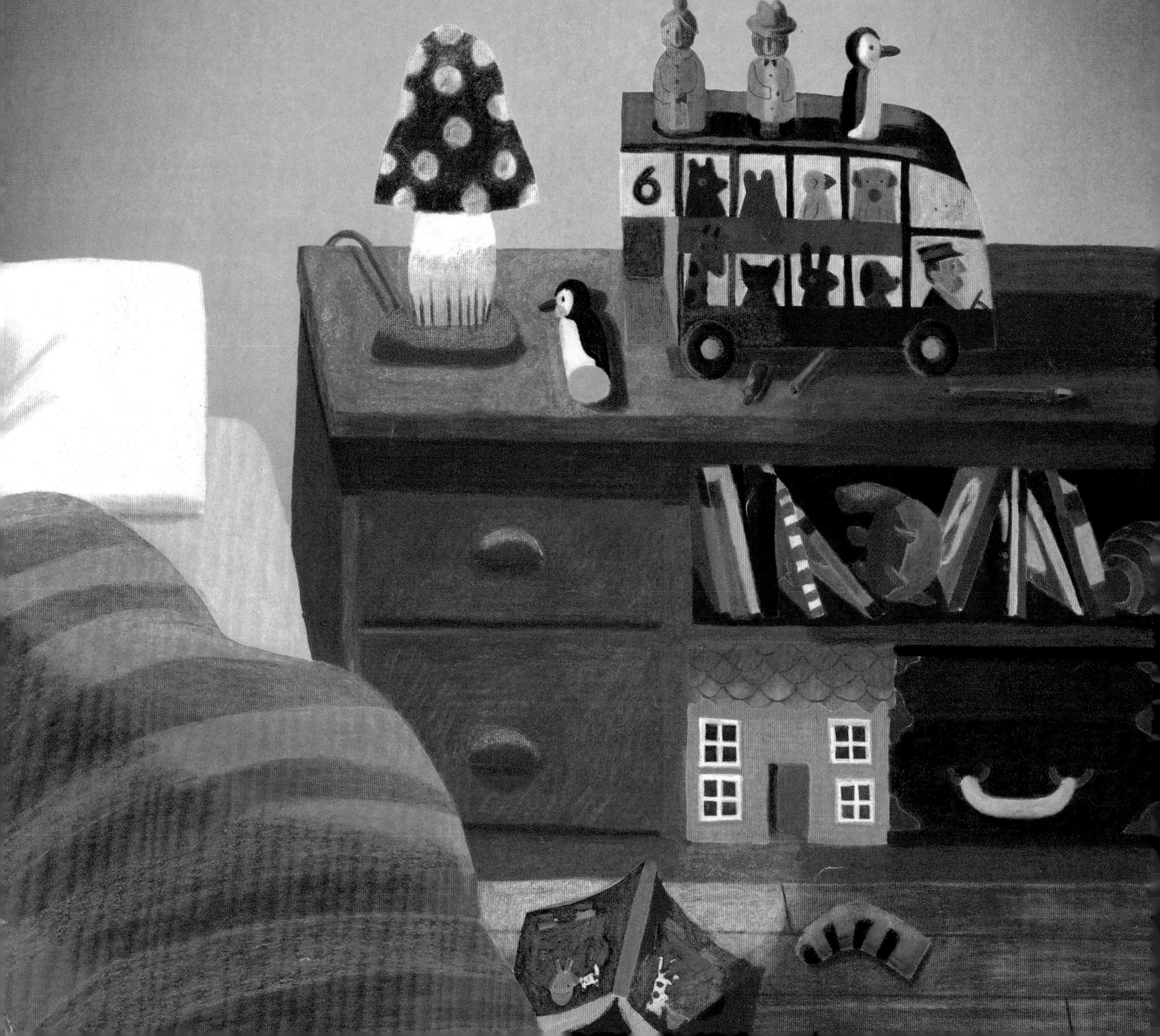
6

"Who are the Terrible Two?" said Elmer.

"Look," said Dad. "There's Filth. He pours muck and slime over everything."

"And there's Vacuum," said Emily.

"He can suck money and jewels and treasure out of people's pockets, out of drawers, even out of banks," said Dad.

"Wow!" said Elmer.

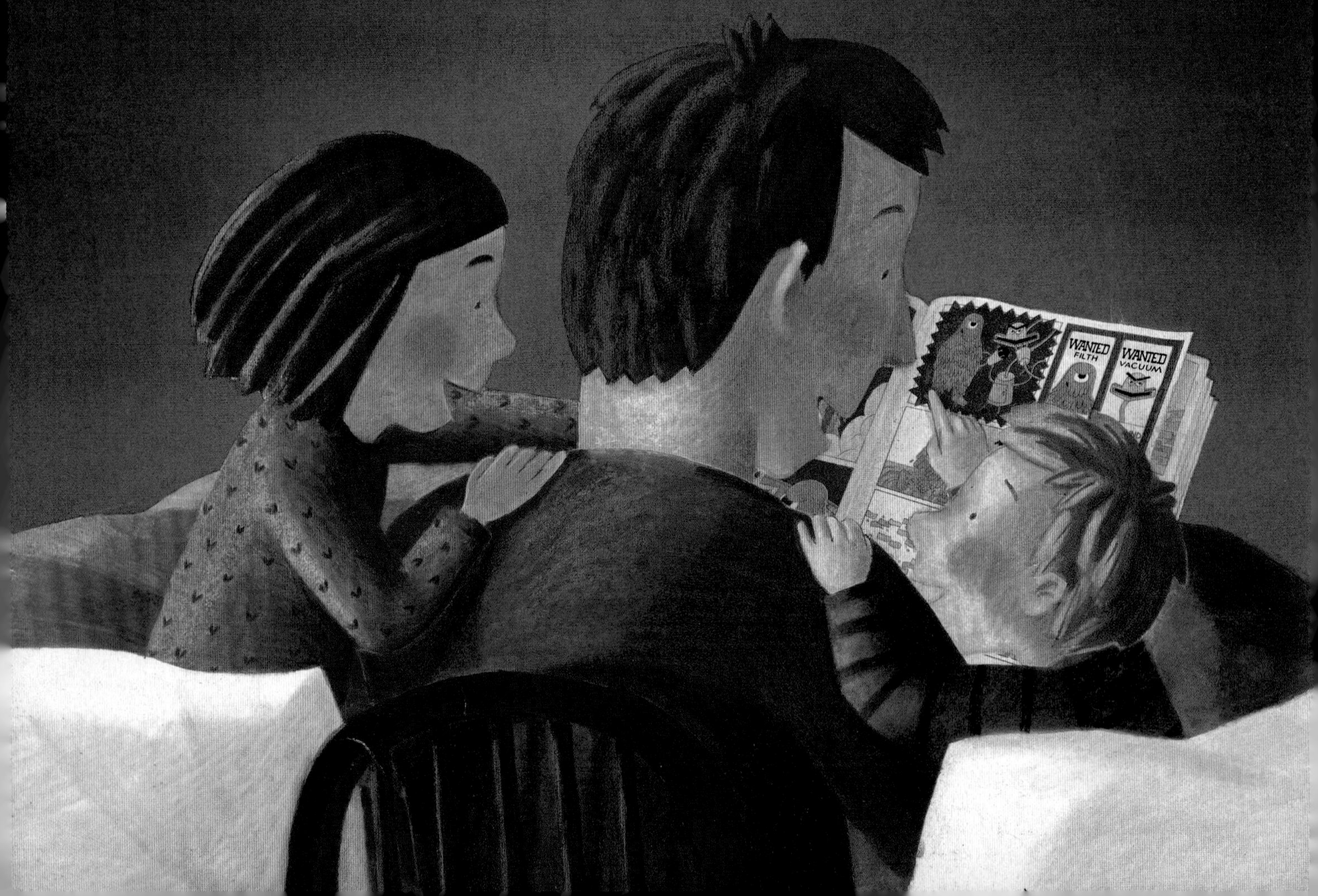
WANTED
FILTH
WANTED
VACUUM

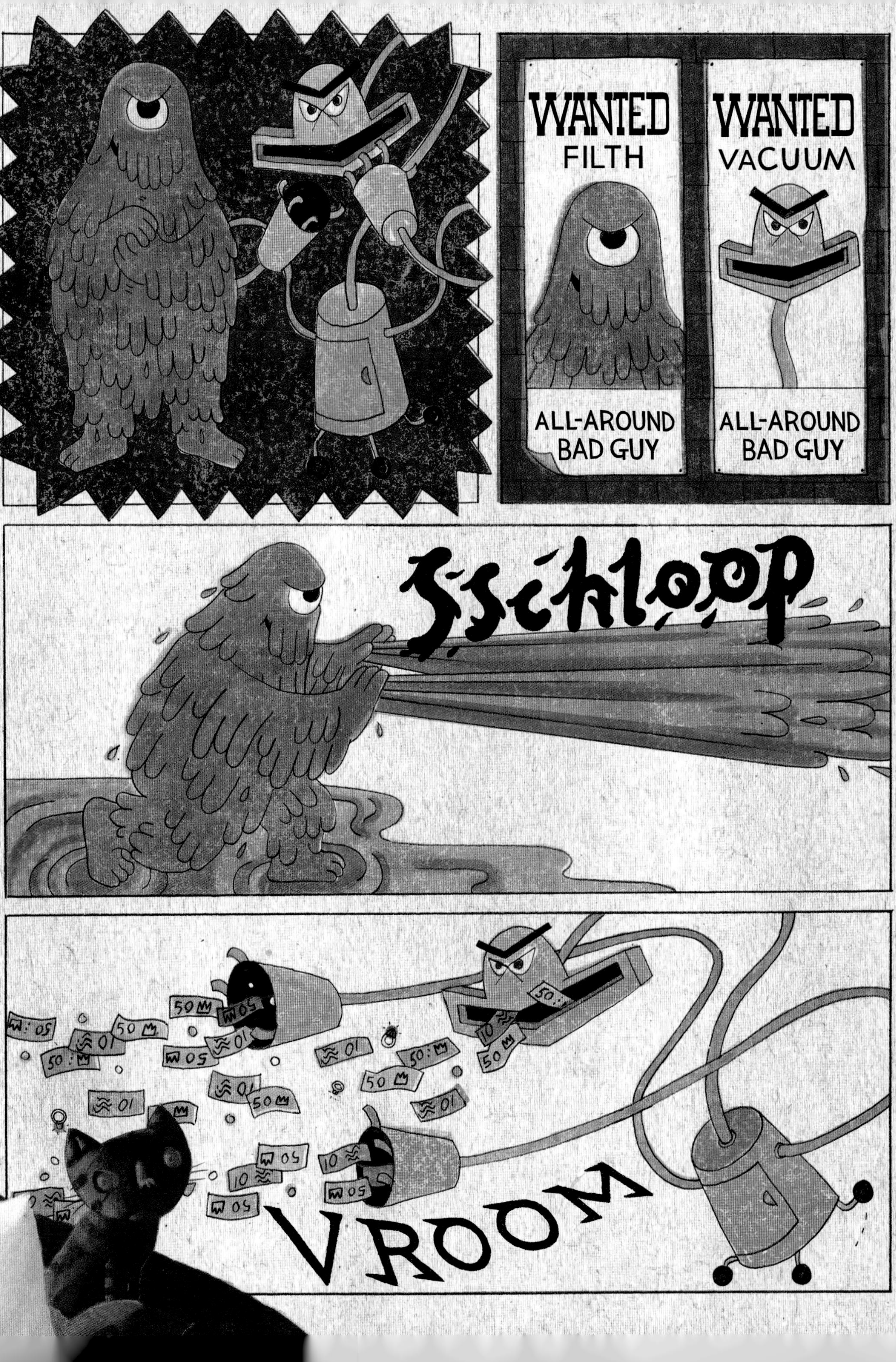
WANTED
FILTH
ALL-AROUND BAD GUY
WANTED
VACUUM
ALL-AROUND BAD GUY
SSCHLOOP
VROOM

Dad went on. . . .

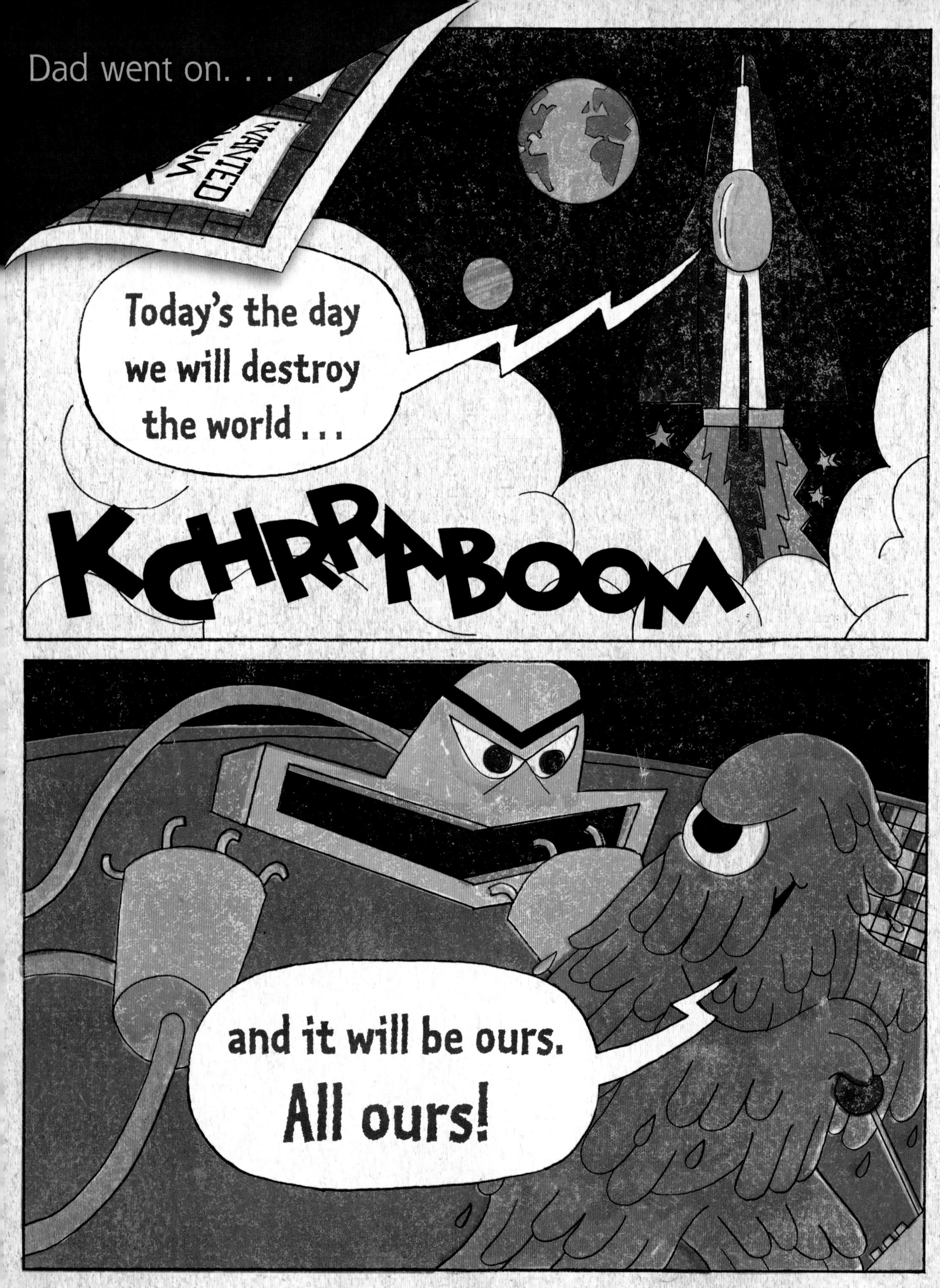
WANTED
Today's the day we will destroy the world . . .
KCHRRABOOM
and it will be ours.
All ours!

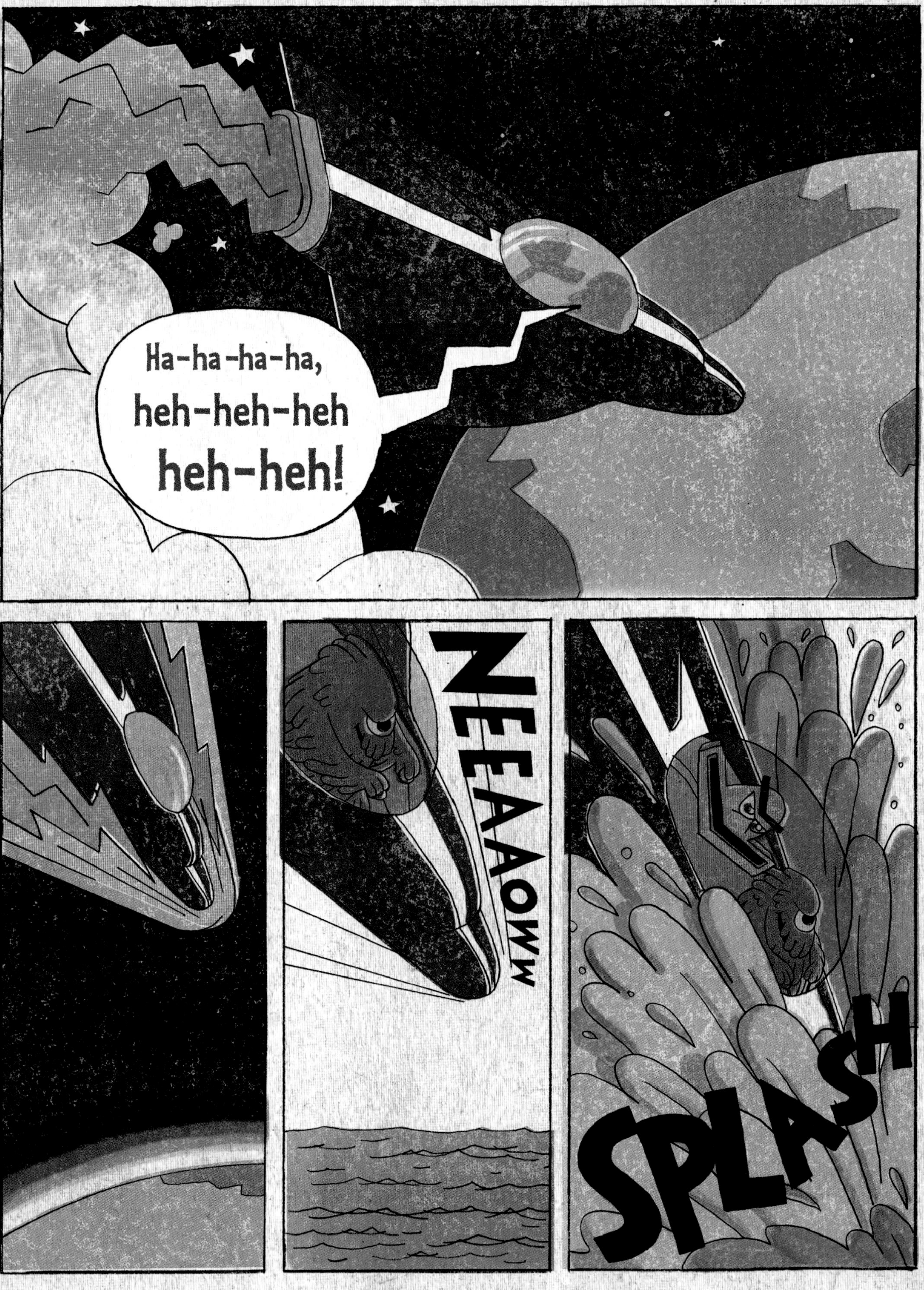

Ha-ha-ha-ha, heh-heh-heh heh-heh!
NEEAAAOWW
SPLASH

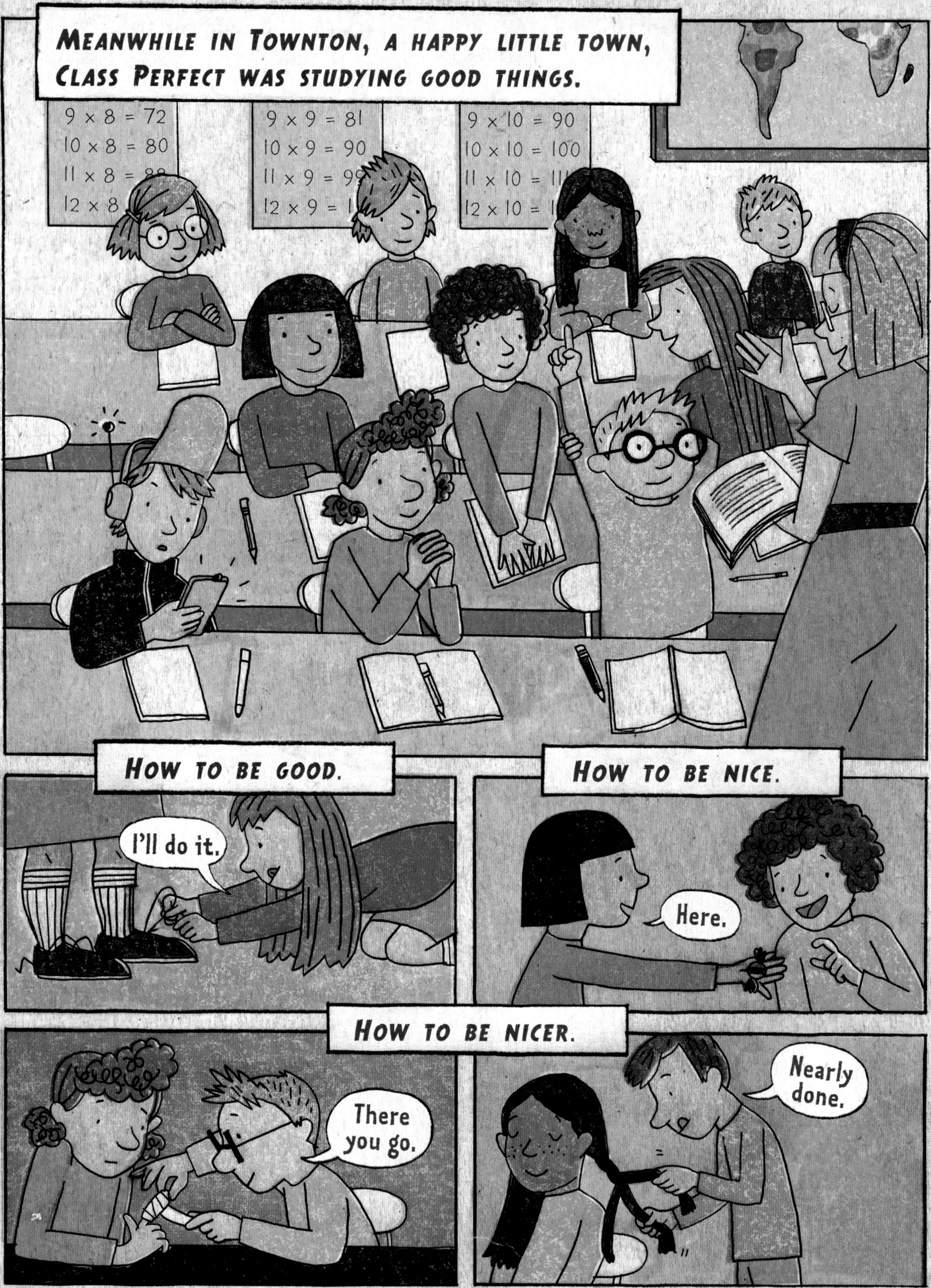
MEANWHILE IN TOWNTON, A HAPPY LITTLE TOWN, CLASS PERFECT WAS STUDYING GOOD THINGS.
9 × 8 = 72
10 × 8 = 80
9 × 9 = 81
10 × 9 = 90
9 × 10 = 90
10 × 10 = 100
HOW TO BE GOOD.
I'll do it.
HOW TO BE NICE.
Here.
HOW TO BE NICER.
There you go.
Nearly done.

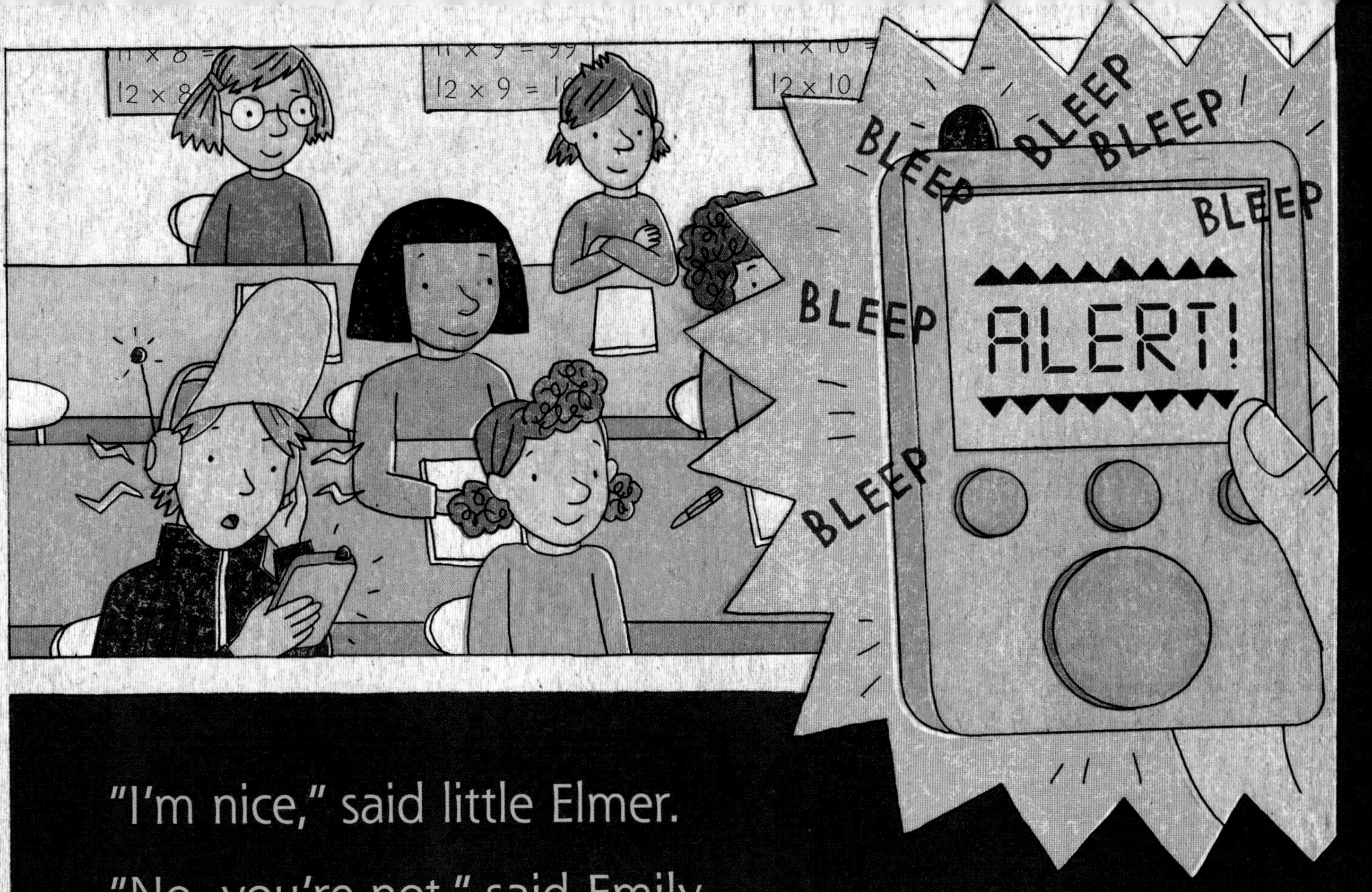
BLEEP
BLEEP
BLEEP
BLEEP
BLEEP
BLEEP
ALERT!

"I'm nice," said little Elmer.
"No, you're not," said Emily.
"I am, aren't I, Dad?"
said Elmer.
"You're both very
good," said Dad.

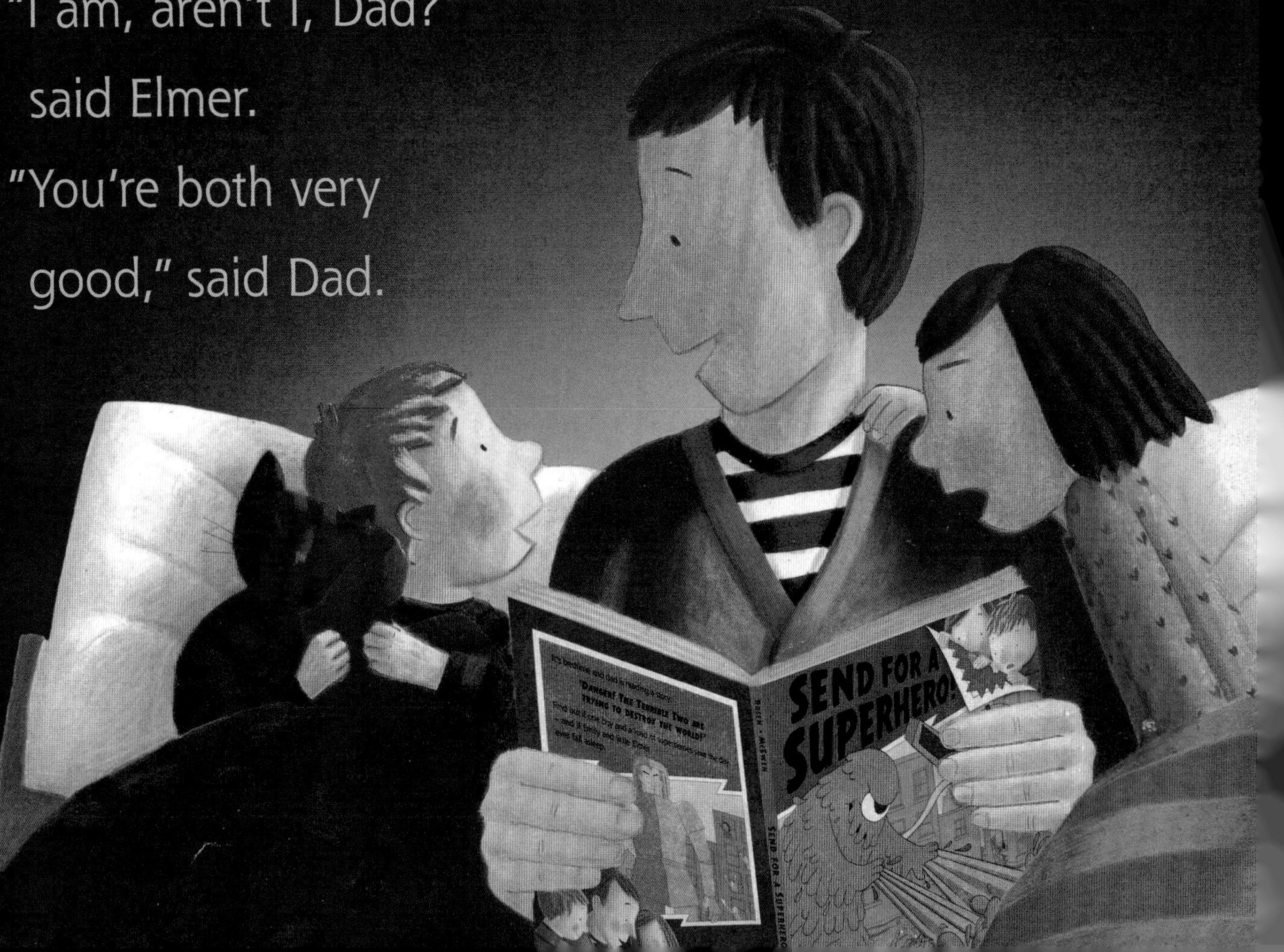
SEND FOR A SUPERHERO!

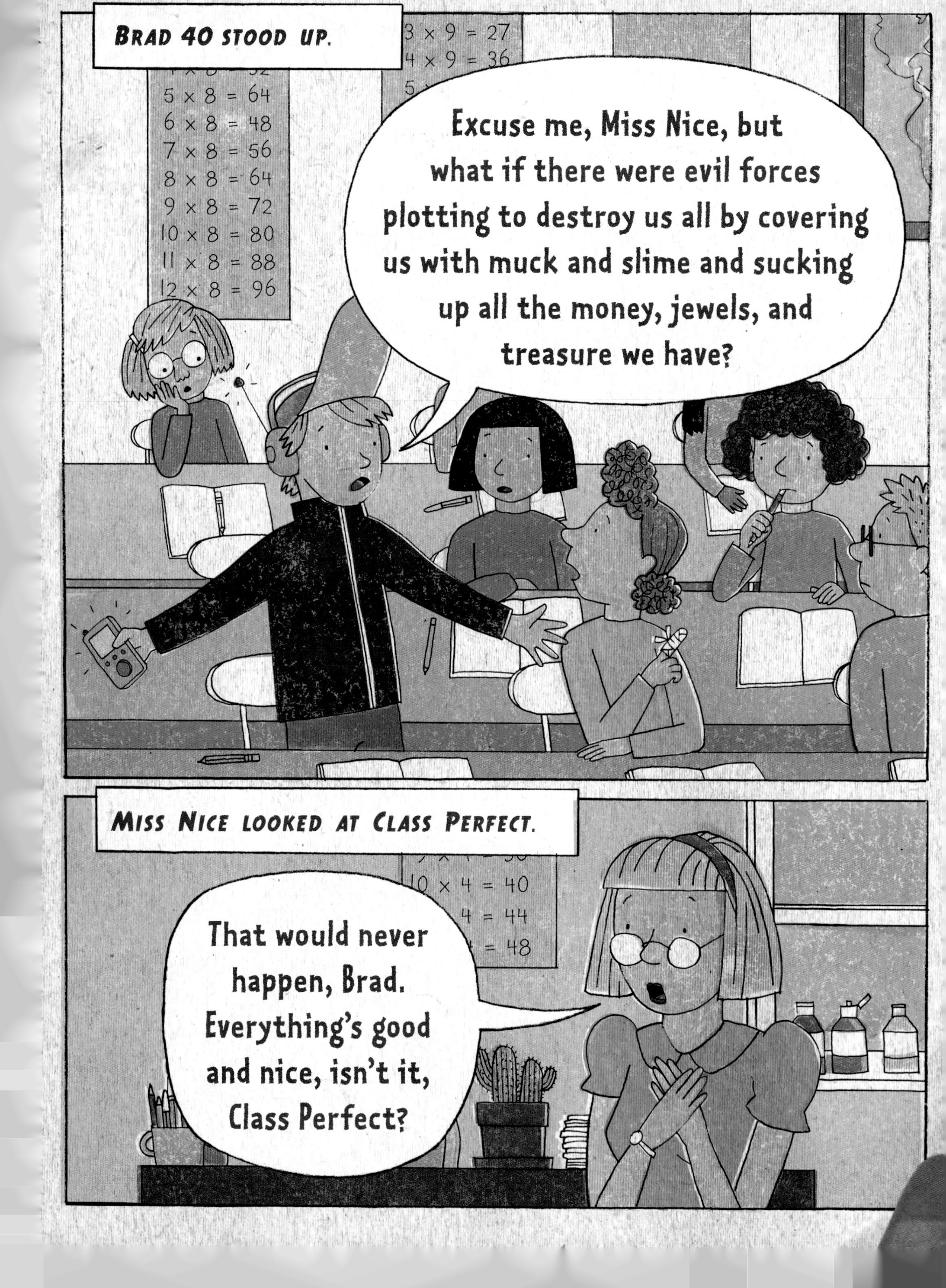
Brad 40 stood up.
3 × 9 = 27
4 × 9 = 36
5 × 8 = 64
6 × 8 = 48
7 × 8 = 56
8 × 8 = 64
9 × 8 = 72
10 × 8 = 80
11 × 8 = 88
12 × 8 = 96
Excuse me, Miss Nice, but what if there were evil forces plotting to destroy us all by covering us with muck and slime and sucking up all the money, jewels, and treasure we have?
Miss Nice looked at Class Perfect.
10 × 4 = 40
That would never happen, Brad. Everything's good and nice, isn't it, Class Perfect?

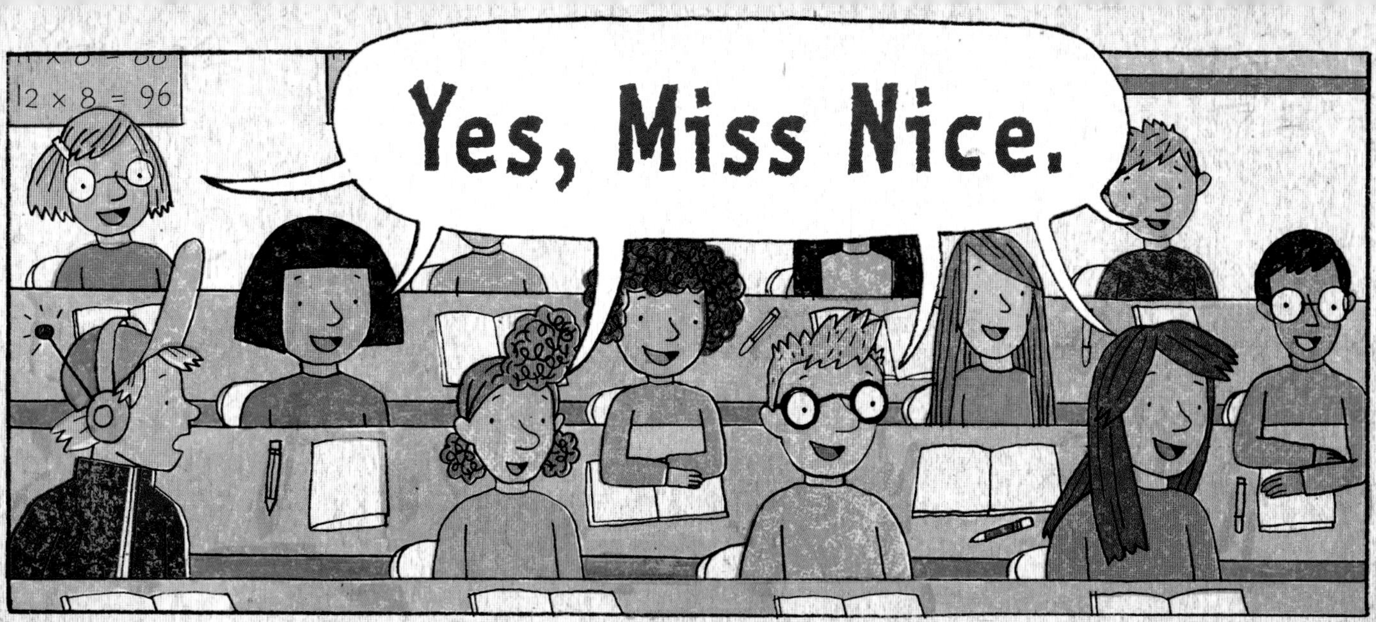
12 × 8 = 96
Yes, Miss Nice.

Emily said, "Brad 40 knows what's going on, doesn't he, Dad?"

Little Elmer jumped up.

"I'm Brad 40!"

"No, you're not," said Emily.

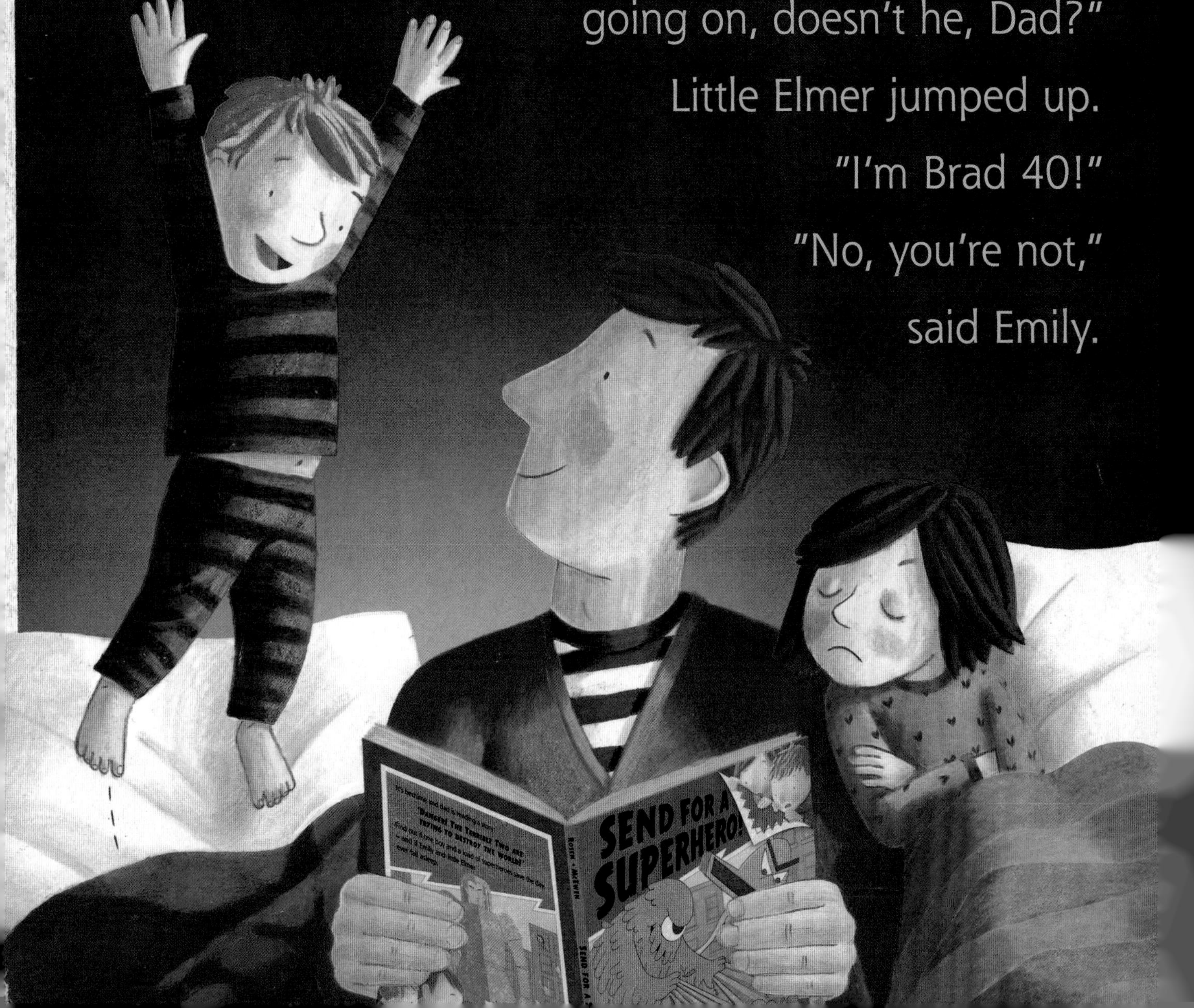
SEND FOR A SUPERHERO!

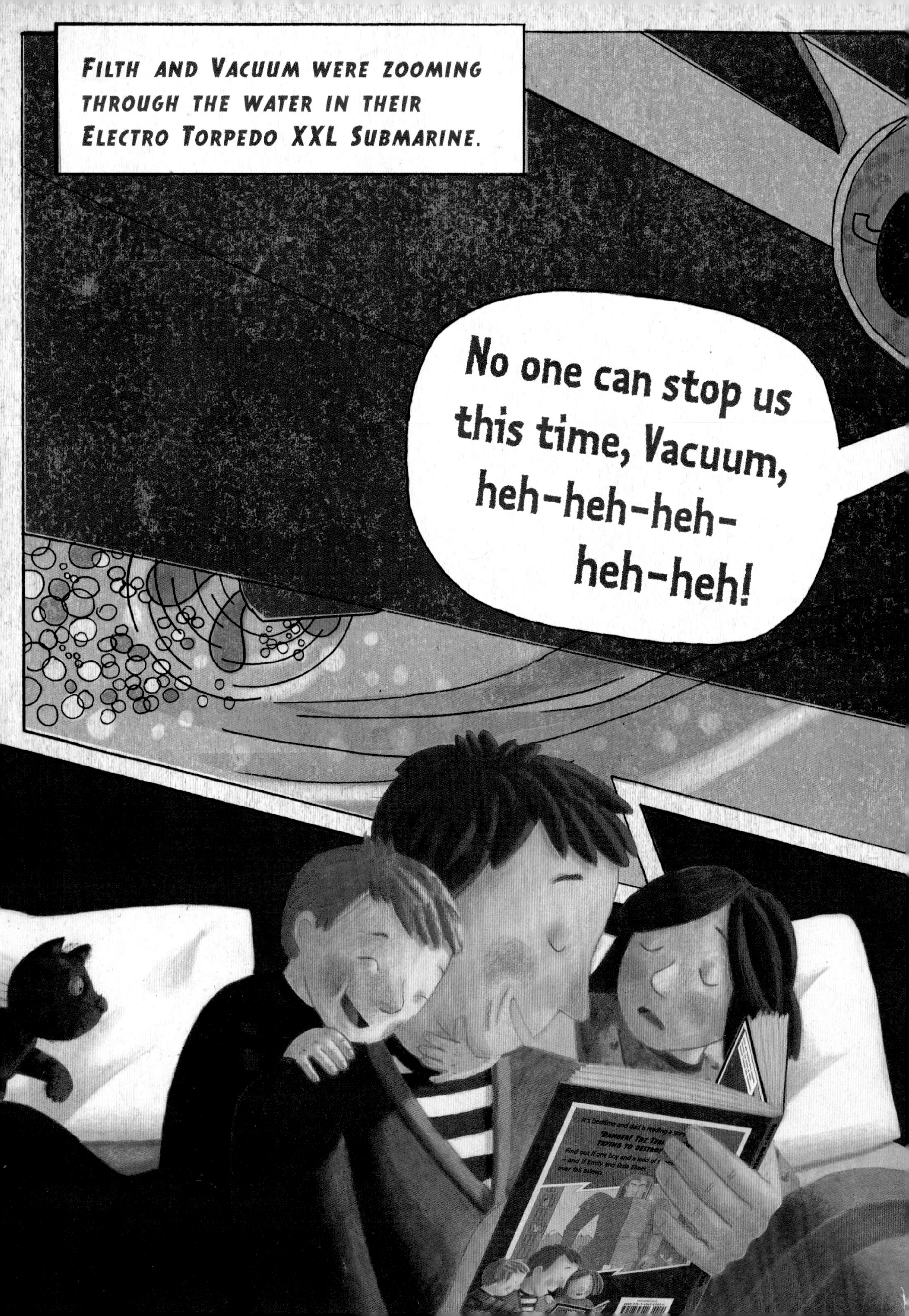
FILTH AND VACUUM WERE ZOOMING THROUGH THE WATER IN THEIR ELECTRO TORPEDO XXL SUBMARINE.
No one can stop us this time, Vacuum, heh-heh-heh-heh-heh!

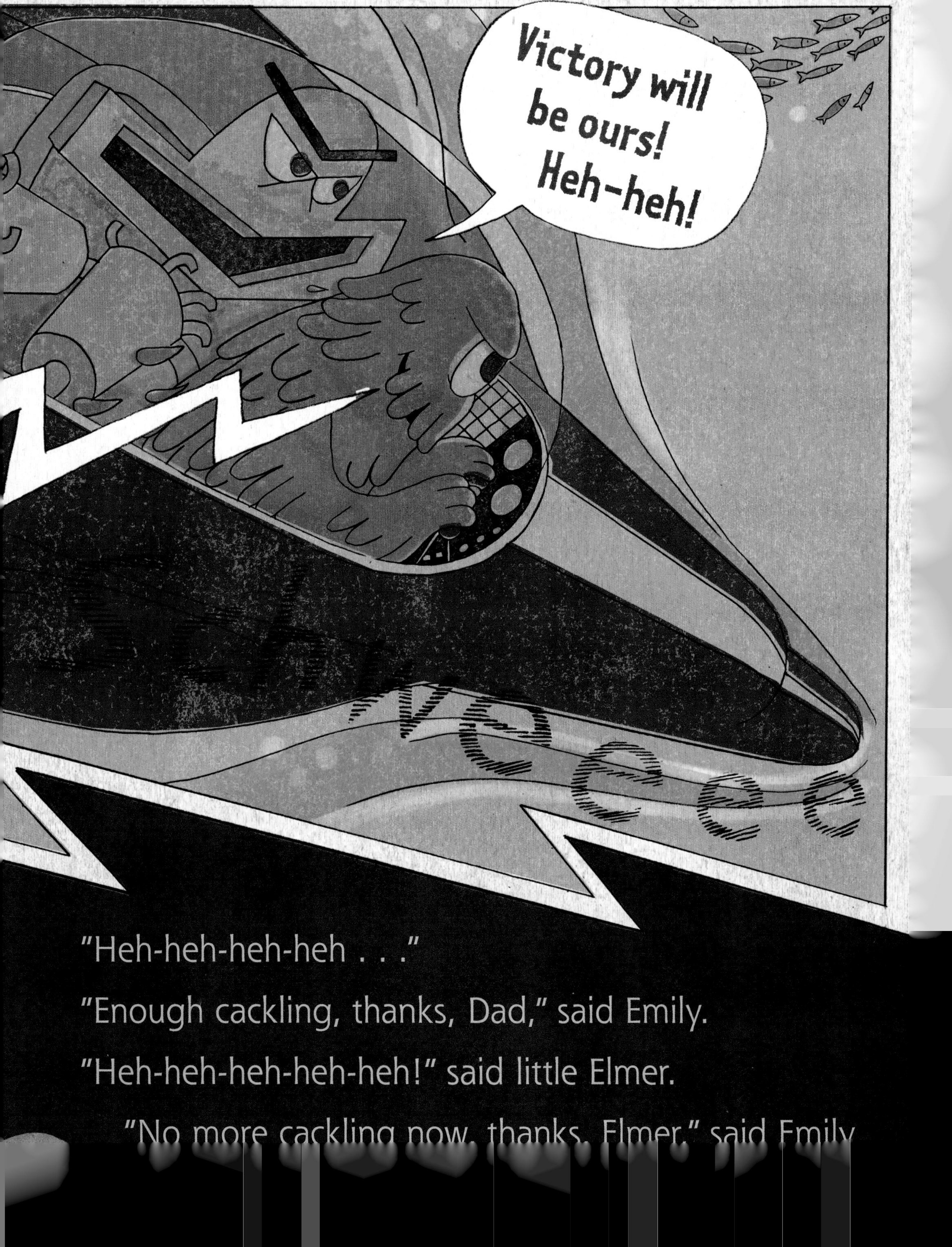
Victory will be ours! Heh-heh!

"Heh-heh-heh-heh . . ."

"Enough cackling, thanks, Dad," said Emily.

"Heh-heh-heh-heh-heh!" said little Elmer.

"No more cackling now, thanks, Elmer," said Emily

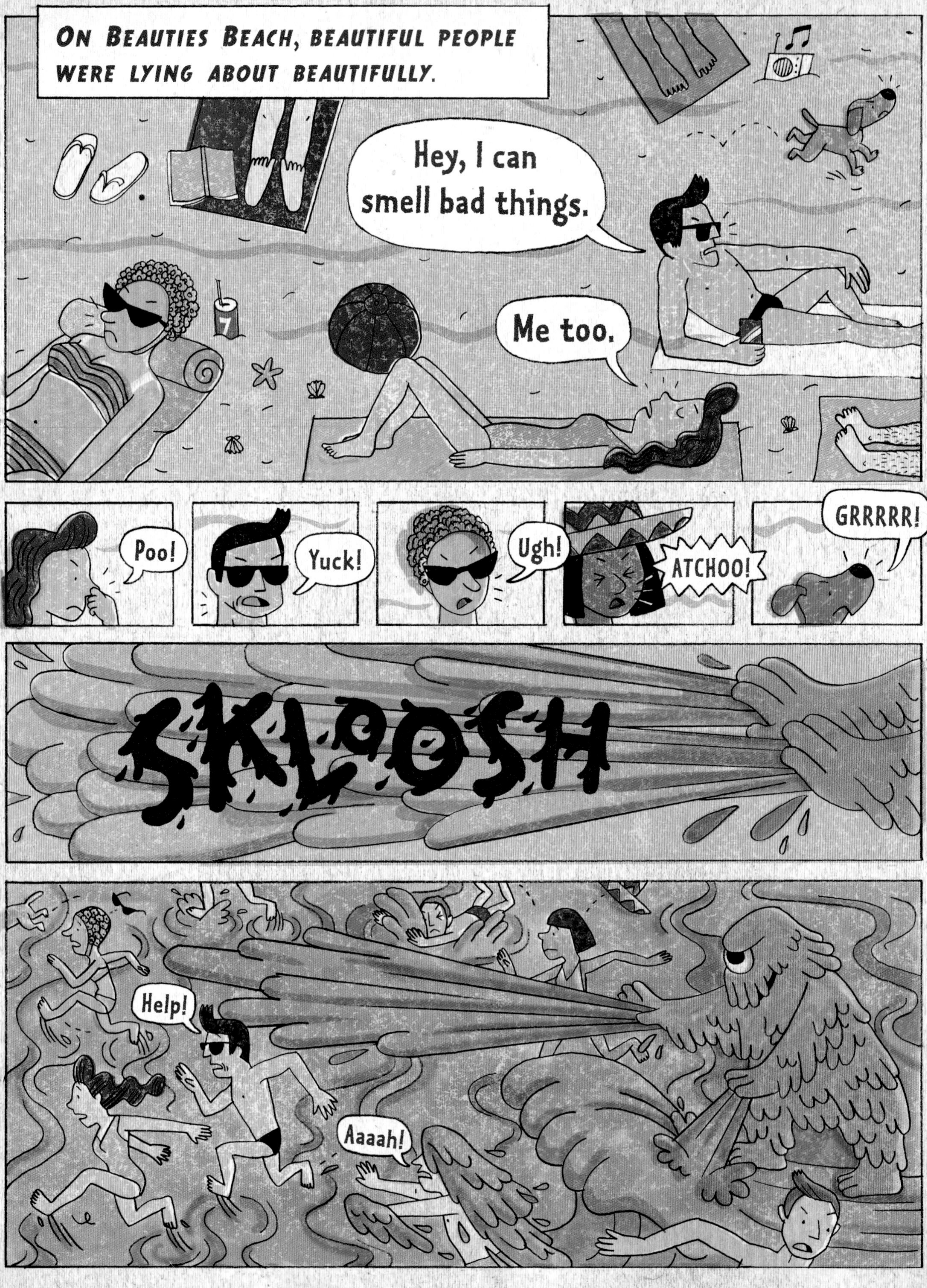
ON BEAUTIES BEACH, BEAUTIFUL PEOPLE WERE LYING ABOUT BEAUTIFULLY.
Hey, I can smell bad things.
Me too.
Poo!
Yuck!
Ugh!
ATCHOO!
GRRRRR!
SKLOOSH
Help!
Aaaah!

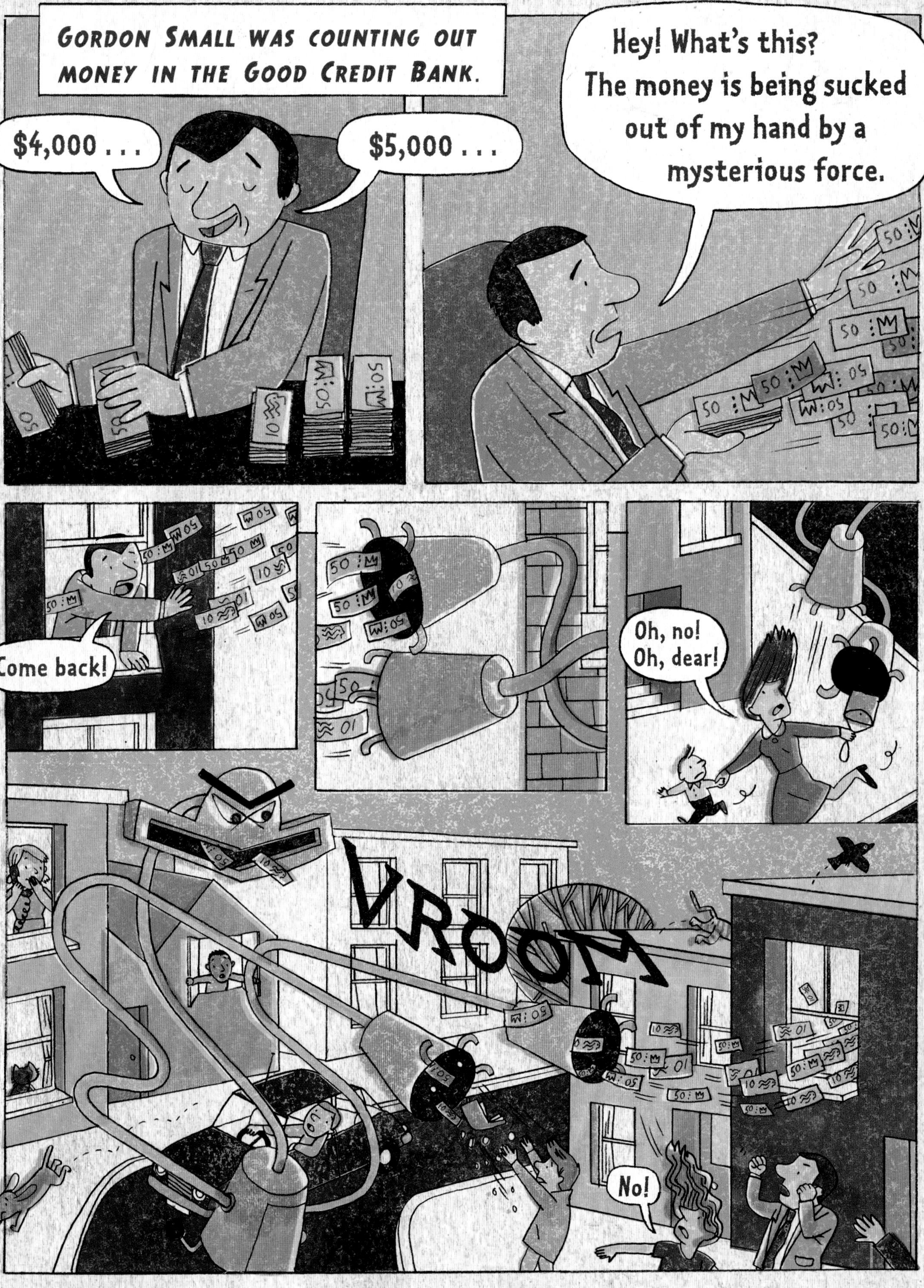
GORDON SMALL WAS COUNTING OUT MONEY IN THE GOOD CREDIT BANK.
$4,000 . . .
$5,000 . . .
Hey! What's this? The money is being sucked out of my hand by a mysterious force.
Come back!
Oh, no! Oh, dear!
VROOM
No!

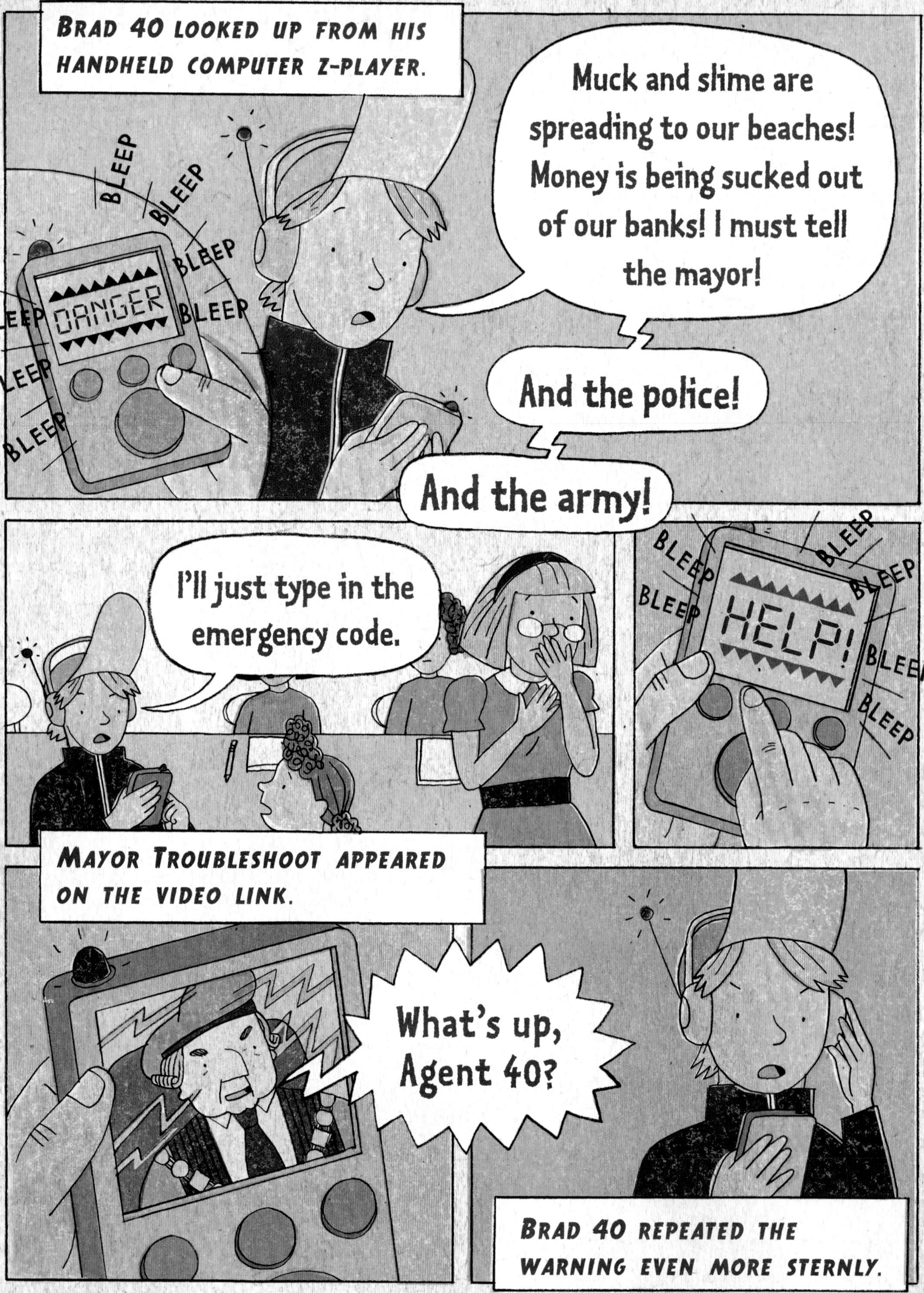
BRAD 40 LOOKED UP FROM HIS HANDHELD COMPUTER Z-PLAYER.
BLEEP BLEEP BLEEP BLEEP BLEEP BLEEP BLEEP
DANGER
Muck and slime are spreading to our beaches! Money is being sucked out of our banks! I must tell the mayor!
And the police!
And the army!
I'll just type in the emergency code.
BLEEP BLEEP BLEEP BLEEP BLEEP BLEEP
HELP!
MAYOR TROUBLESHOOT APPEARED ON THE VIDEO LINK.
What's up, Agent 40?
BRAD 40 REPEATED THE WARNING EVEN MORE STERNLY.

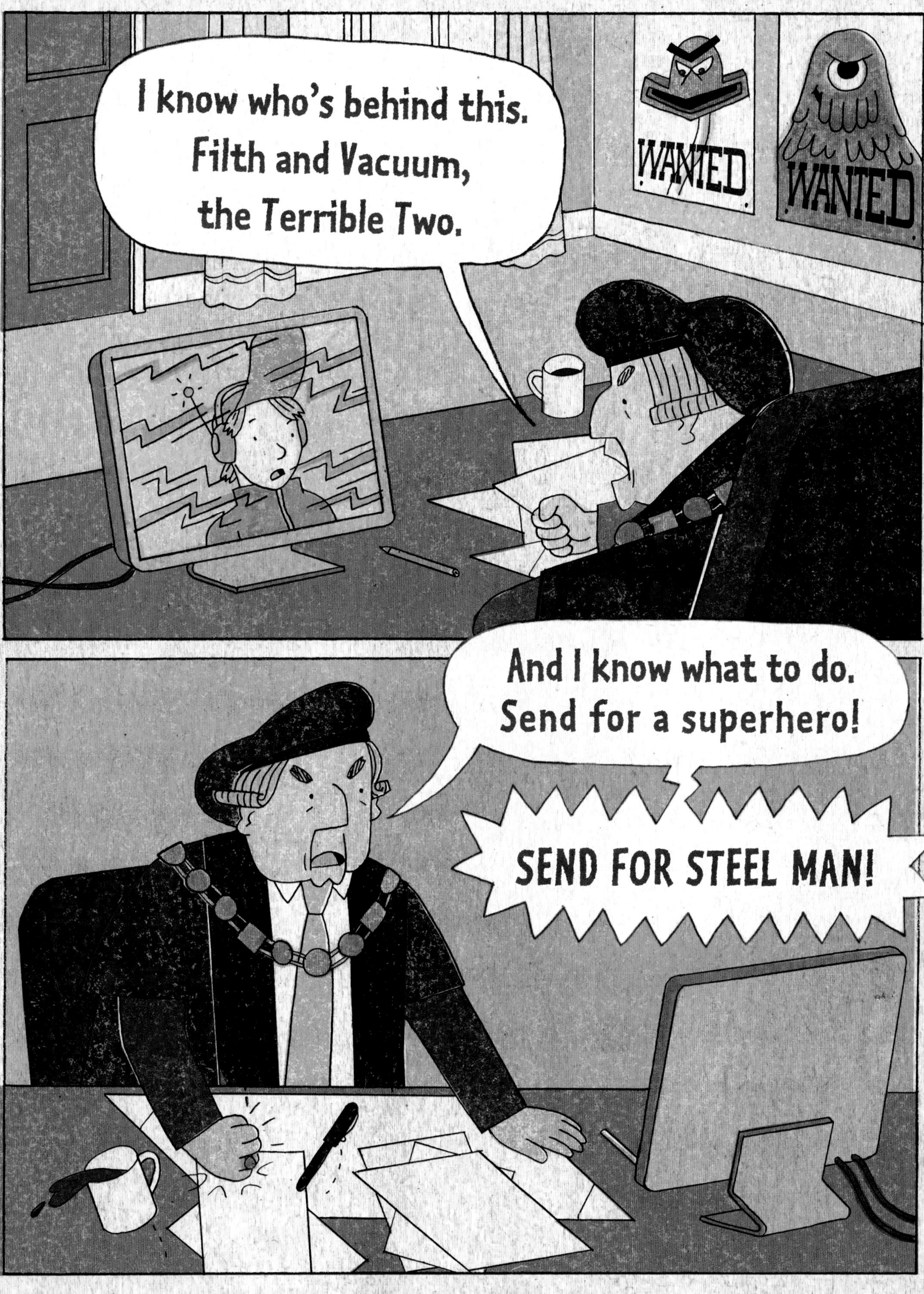
I know who's behind this. Filth and Vacuum, the Terrible Two.
WANTED
WANTED
And I know what to do. Send for a superhero!
SEND FOR STEEL MAN!

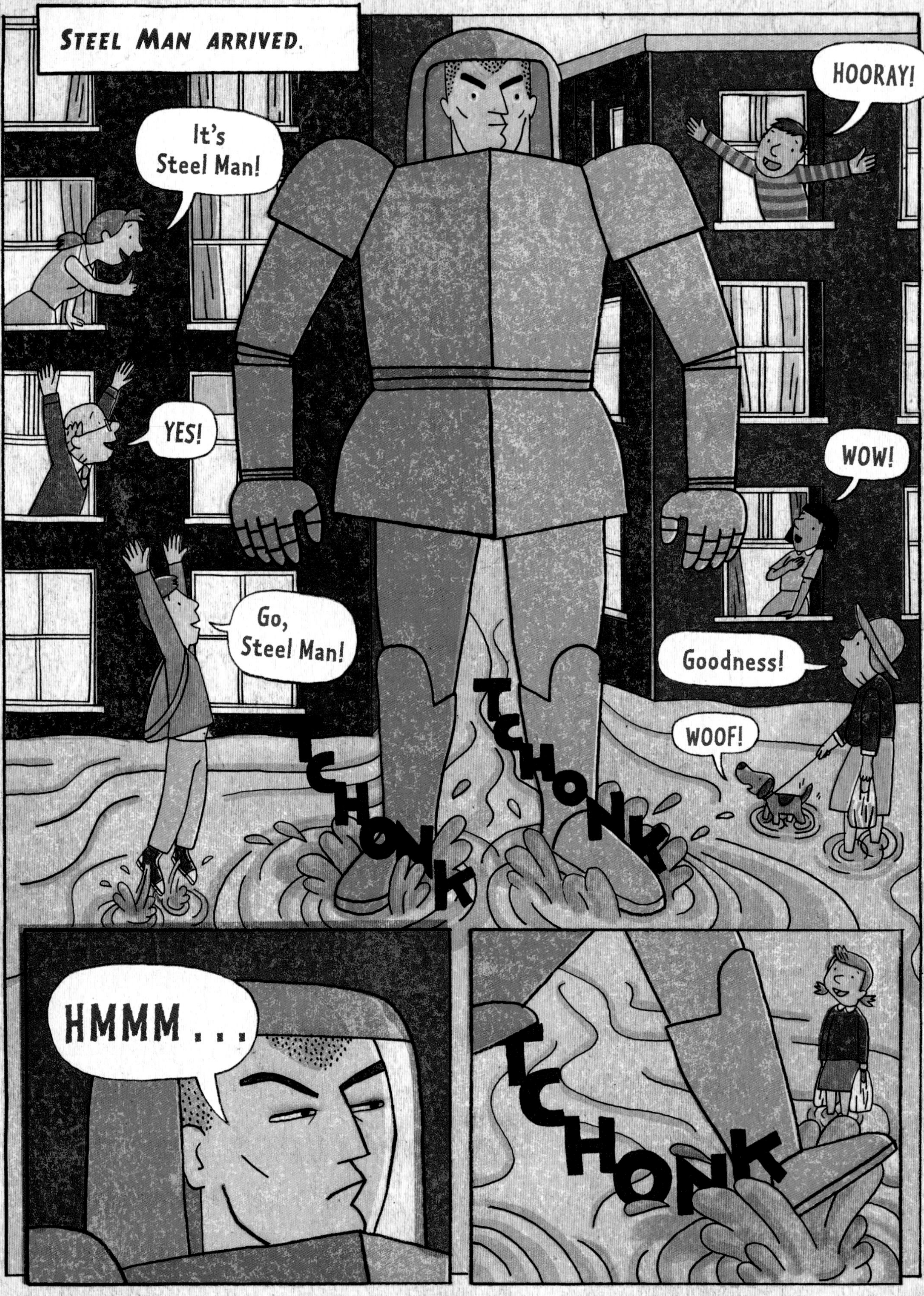
STEEL MAN ARRIVED.
It's Steel Man!
HOORAY!
YES!
WOW!
Go, Steel Man!
Goodness!
WOOF!
TCHONK
TCHONK
HMMM . . .
TCHONK

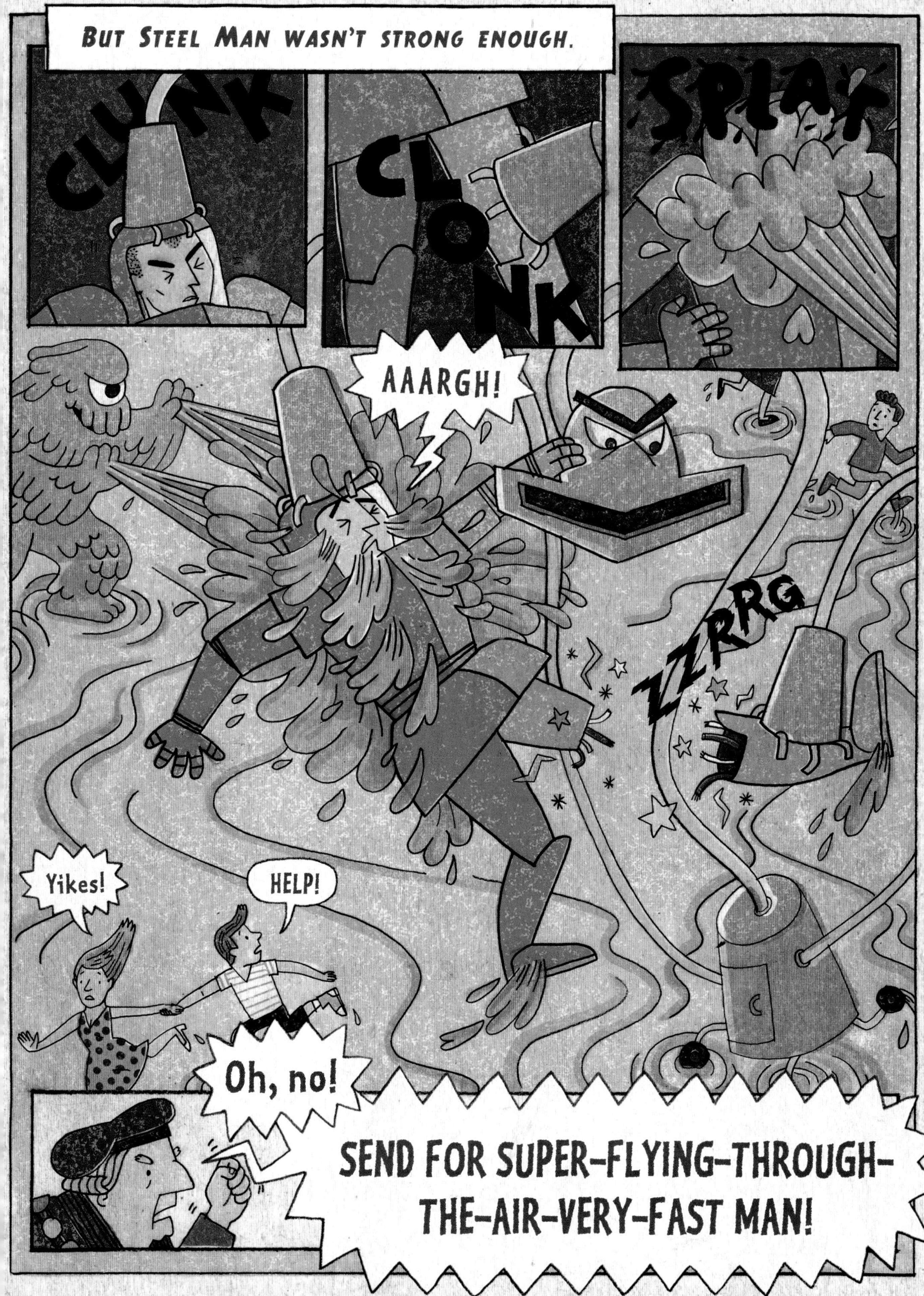

BUT STEEL MAN WASN'T STRONG ENOUGH.
CLUNK
CLONK
SPLAT
AAARGH!
ZZRRG
Yikes!
HELP!
Oh, no!
SEND FOR SUPER-FLYING-THROUGH-THE-AIR-VERY-FAST MAN!

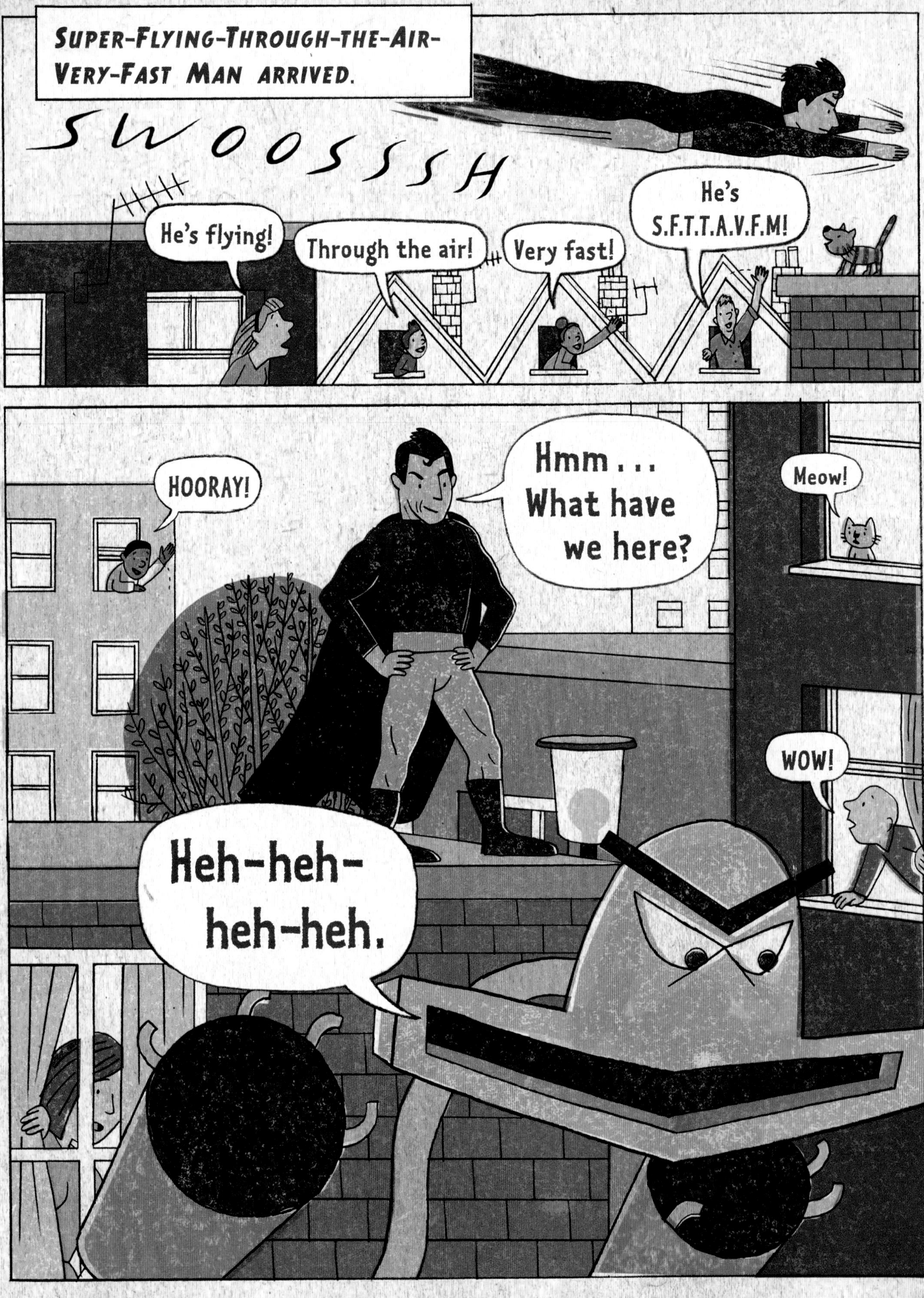
SUPER-FLYING-THROUGH-THE-AIR-VERY-FAST MAN ARRIVED.
SWOOSSSH
He's flying!
Through the air!
Very fast!
He's S.F.T.T.A.V.F.M!
HOORAY!
Hmm . . . What have we here?
Meow!
WOW!
Heh-heh-heh-heh.

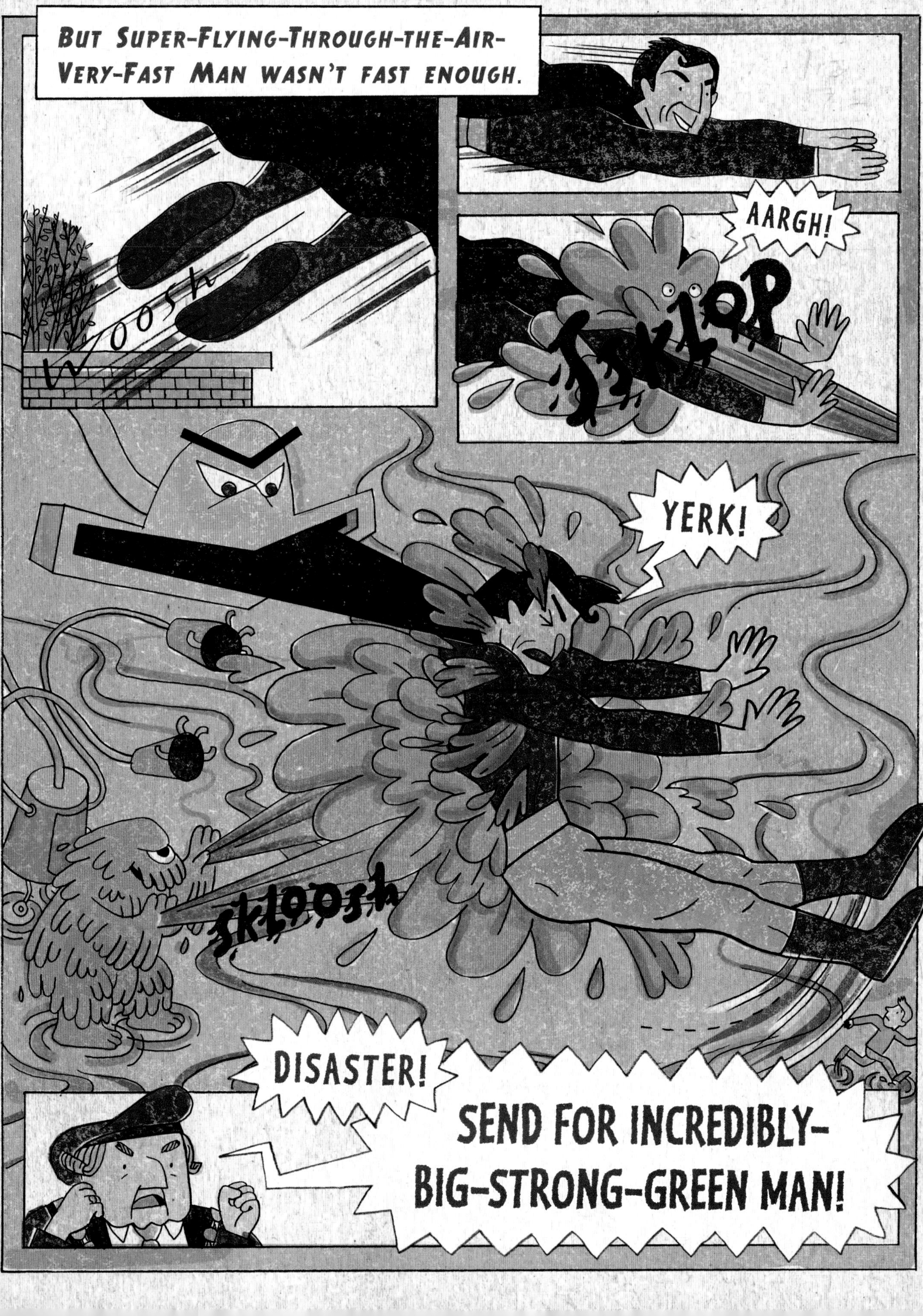
BUT SUPER-FLYING-THROUGH-THE-AIR-VERY-FAST MAN WASN'T FAST ENOUGH.
WOOSH
AARGH!
SKLOP
YERK!
SKLOOSH
DISASTER!
SEND FOR INCREDIBLY-BIG-STRONG-GREEN MAN!

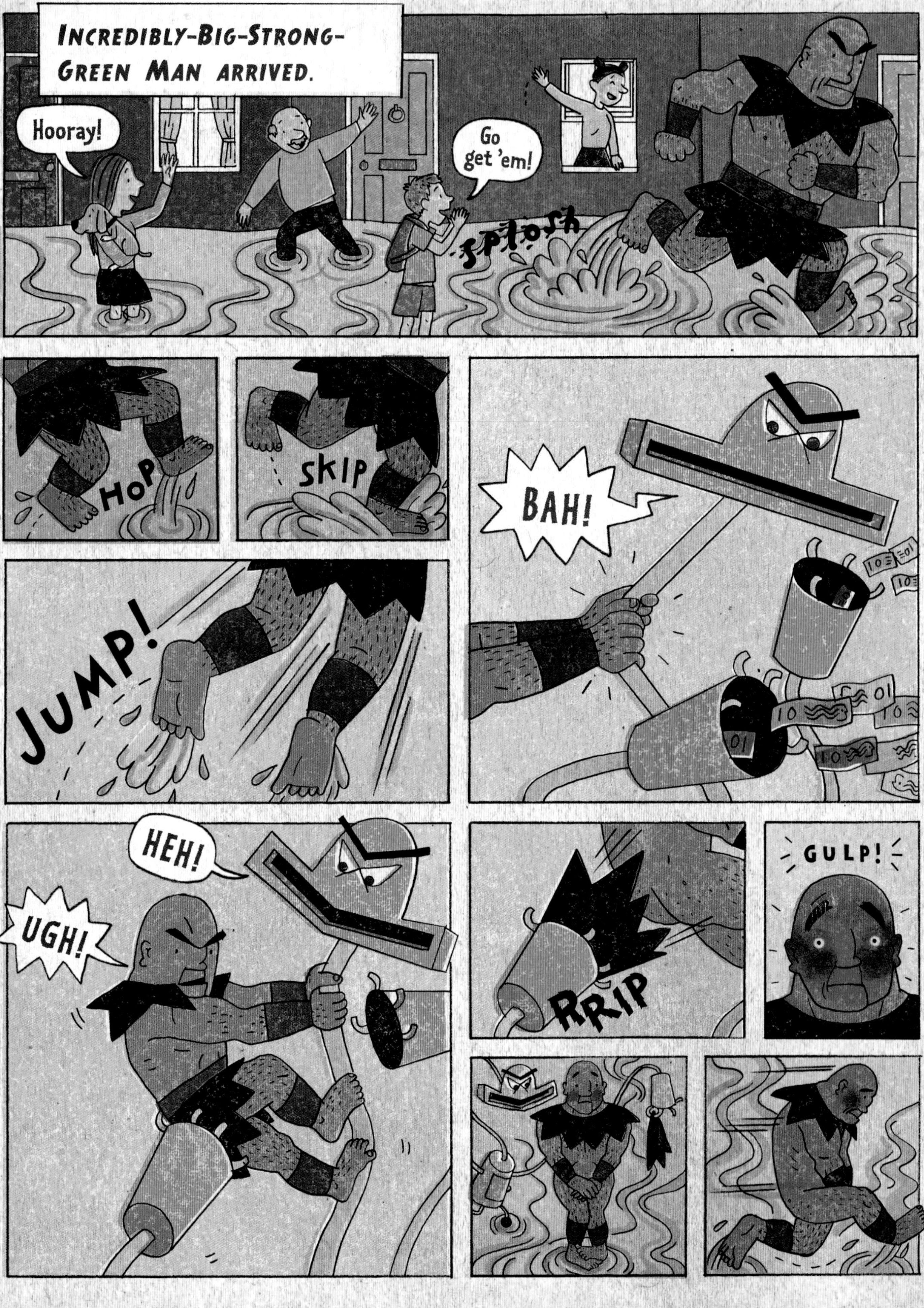
INCREDIBLY-BIG-STRONG-GREEN MAN ARRIVED.
Hooray!
Go get 'em!
SPLOSH
HOP
SKIP
BAH!
JUMP!
HEH!
UGH!
RRIP
GULP!

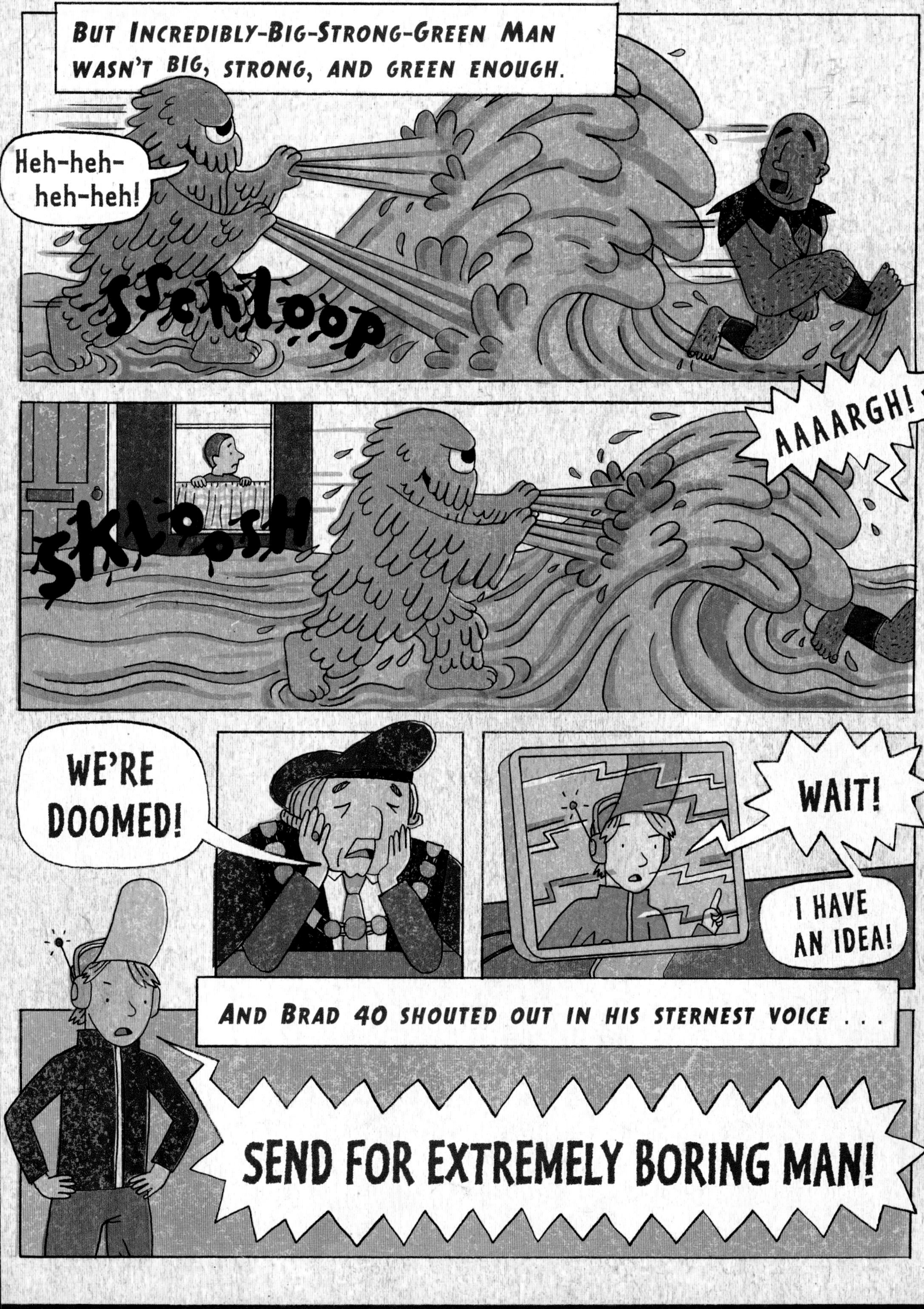
BUT INCREDIBLY-BIG-STRONG-GREEN MAN WASN'T BIG, STRONG, AND GREEN ENOUGH.
Heh-heh-heh-heh!
SSCHLOOP
SKLOOSH
AAAARGH!
WE'RE DOOMED!
WAIT!
I HAVE AN IDEA!
AND BRAD 40 SHOUTED OUT IN HIS STERNEST VOICE . . .
SEND FOR EXTREMELY BORING MAN!

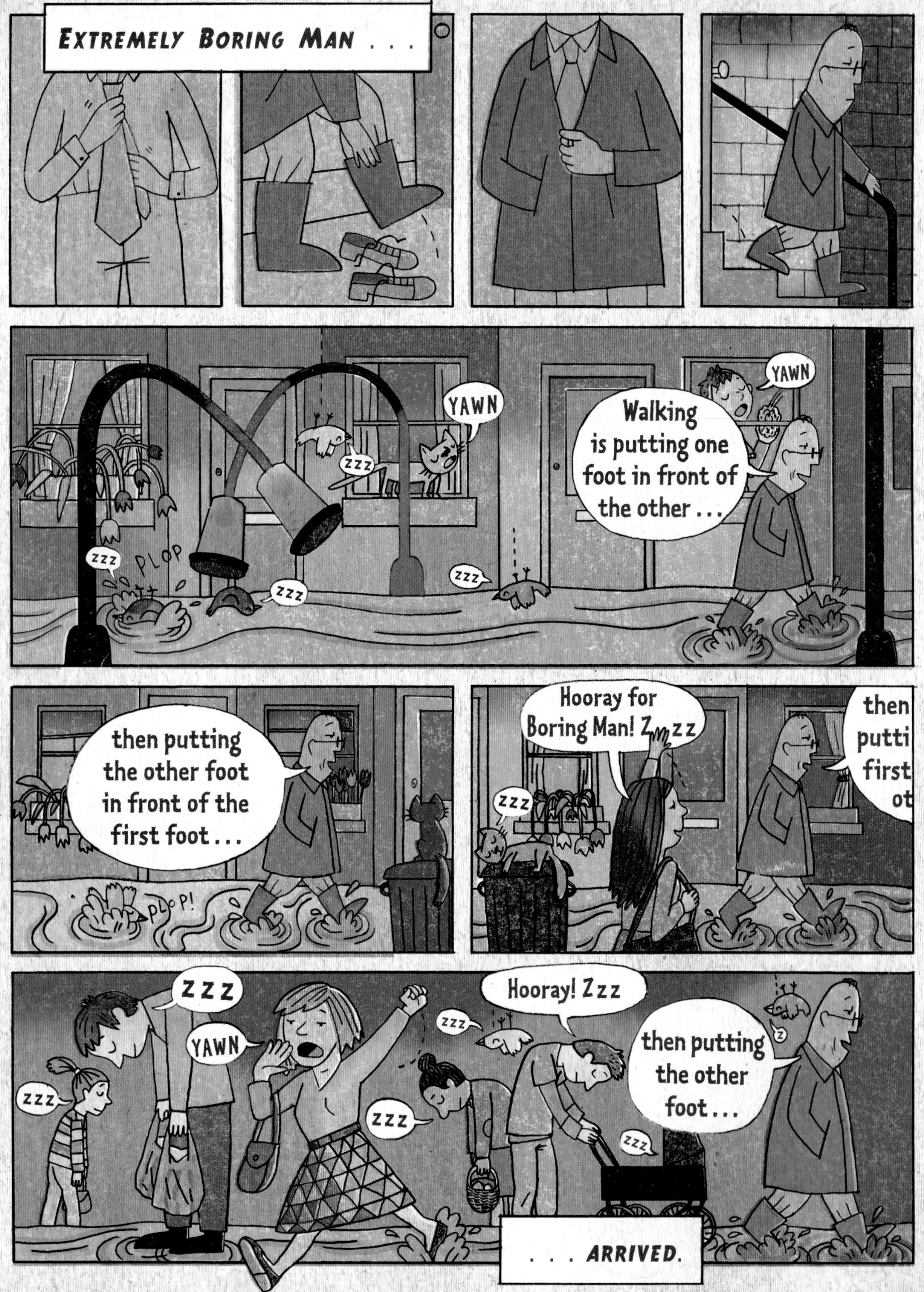
EXTREMELY BORING MAN . . .
YAWN
zzz
Walking is putting one foot in front of the other . . .
YAWN
zzz
PLOP
zzz
zzz
then putting the other foot in front of the first foot . . .
PLOP!
Hooray for Boring Man! Zzz
zzz
ZZZ
YAWN
zzz
zzz
Hooray! Zzz
zzz
zzz
then putting the other foot . . .
z
. . . ARRIVED.

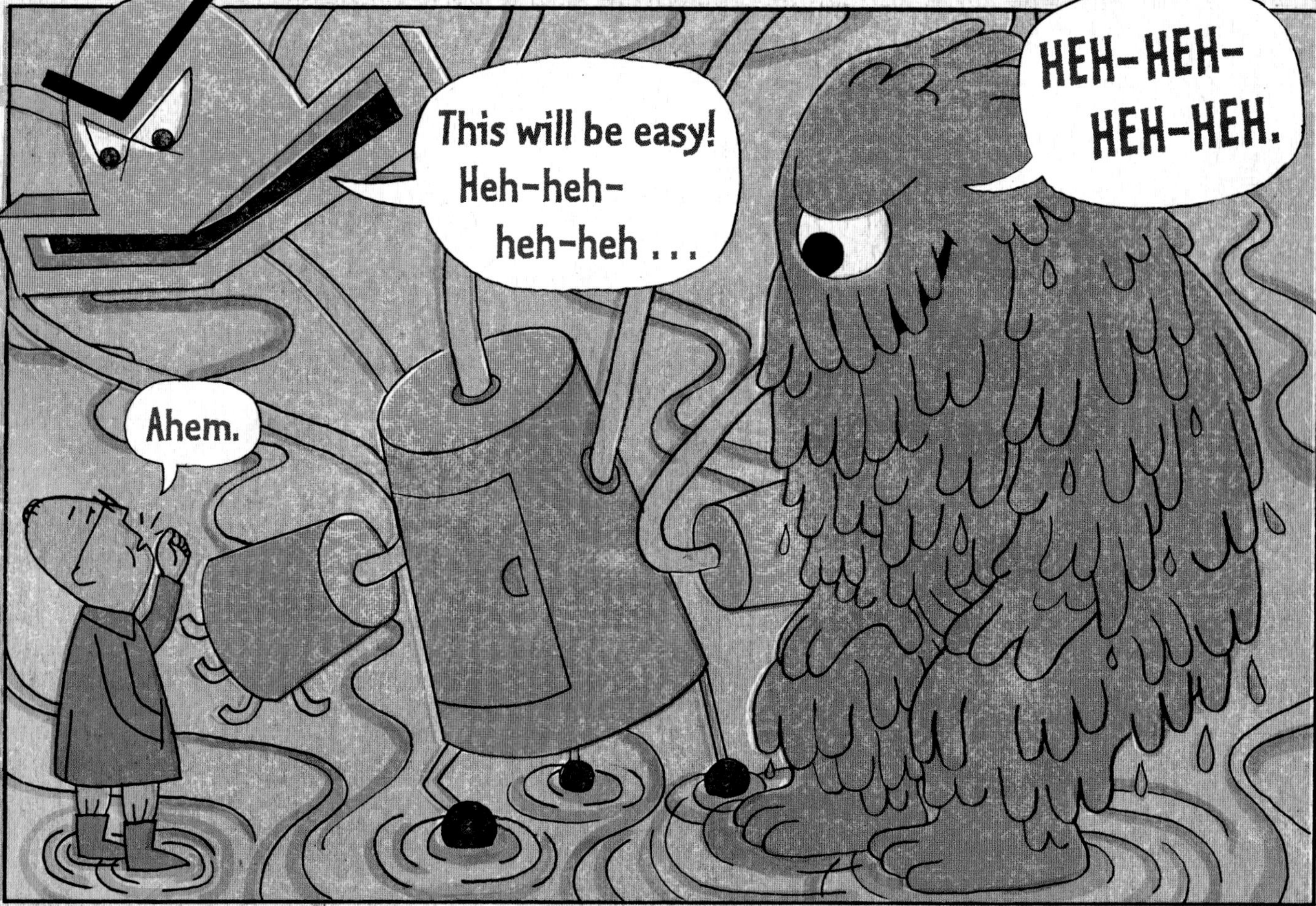
This will be easy! Heh-heh-heh-heh . . .
HEH-HEH-HEH-HEH.
Ahem.

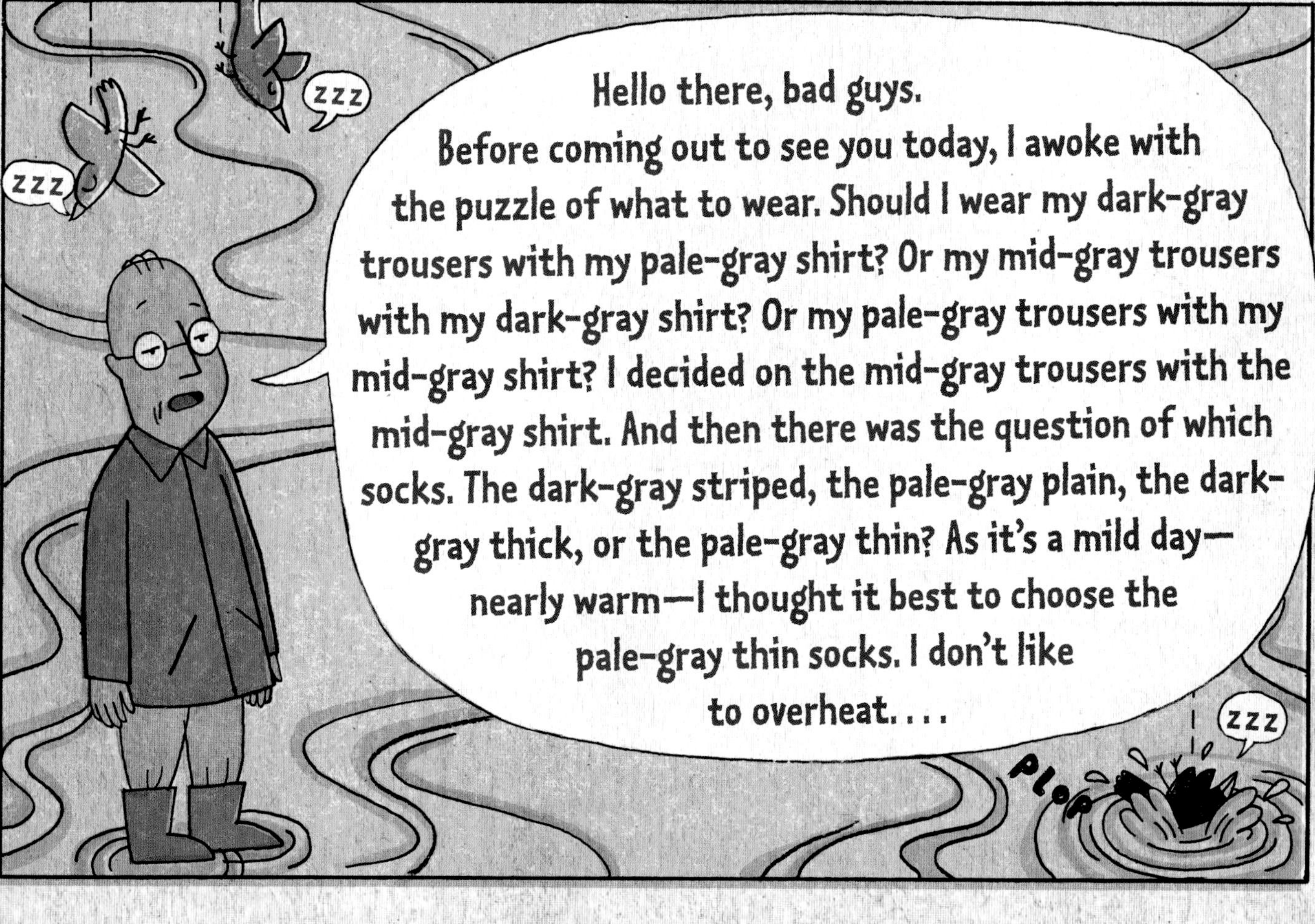
ZZZ
ZZZ
Hello there, bad guys. Before coming out to see you today, I awoke with the puzzle of what to wear. Should I wear my dark-gray trousers with my pale-gray shirt? Or my mid-gray trousers with my dark-gray shirt? Or my pale-gray trousers with my mid-gray shirt? I decided on the mid-gray trousers with the mid-gray shirt. And then there was the question of which socks. The dark-gray striped, the pale-gray plain, the dark-gray thick, or the pale-gray thin? As it's a mild day—nearly warm—I thought it best to choose the pale-gray thin socks. I don't like to overheat. . . .
ZZZ
PLOP

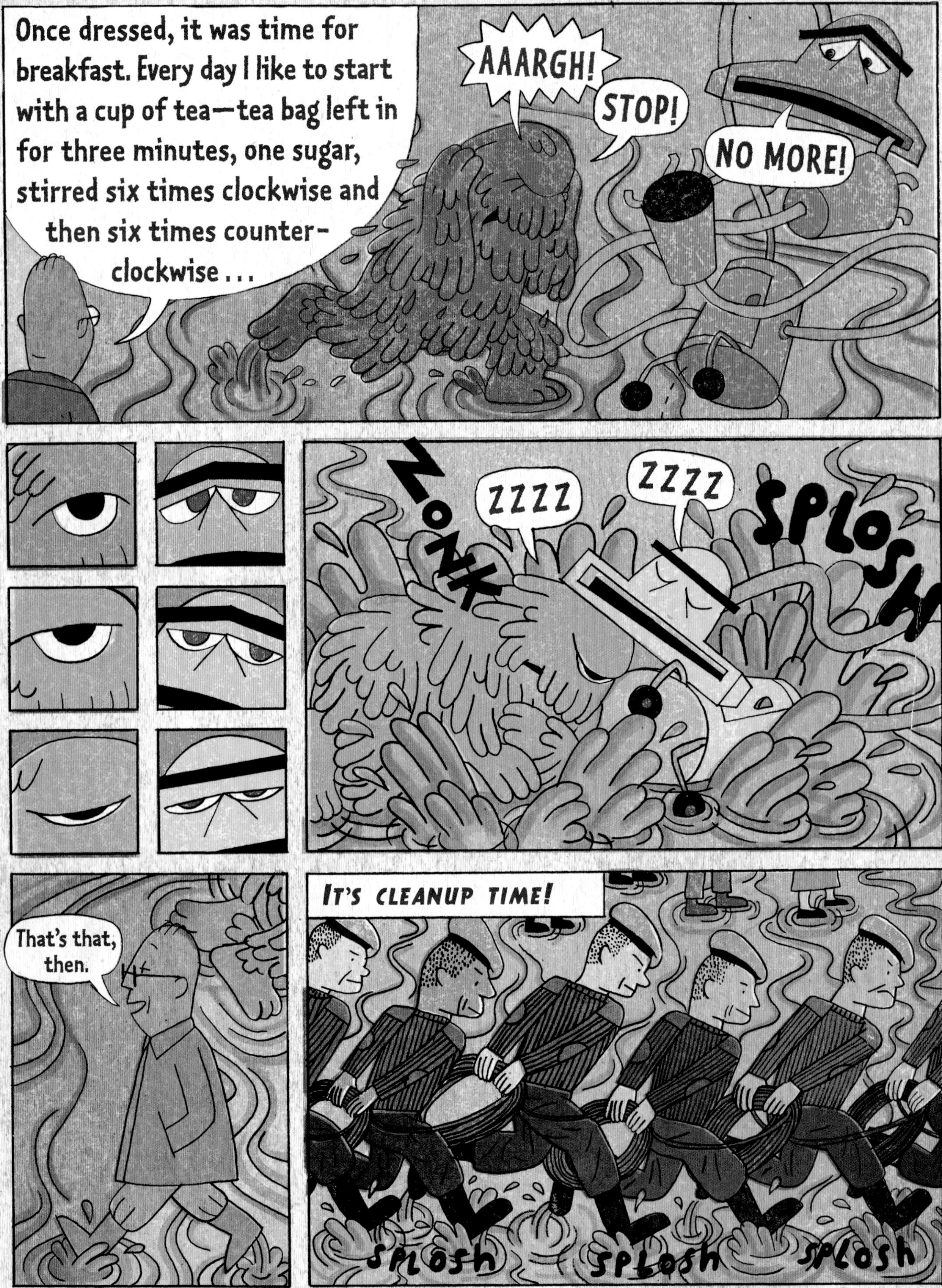

Once dressed, it was time for breakfast. Every day I like to start with a cup of tea—tea bag left in for three minutes, one sugar, stirred six times clockwise and then six times counter-clockwise . . .
AAARGH!
STOP!
NO MORE!
ZONK
ZZZZ
ZZZZ
SPLOSH
That's that, then.
IT'S CLEANUP TIME!
SPLOSH
SPLOSH
SPLOSH

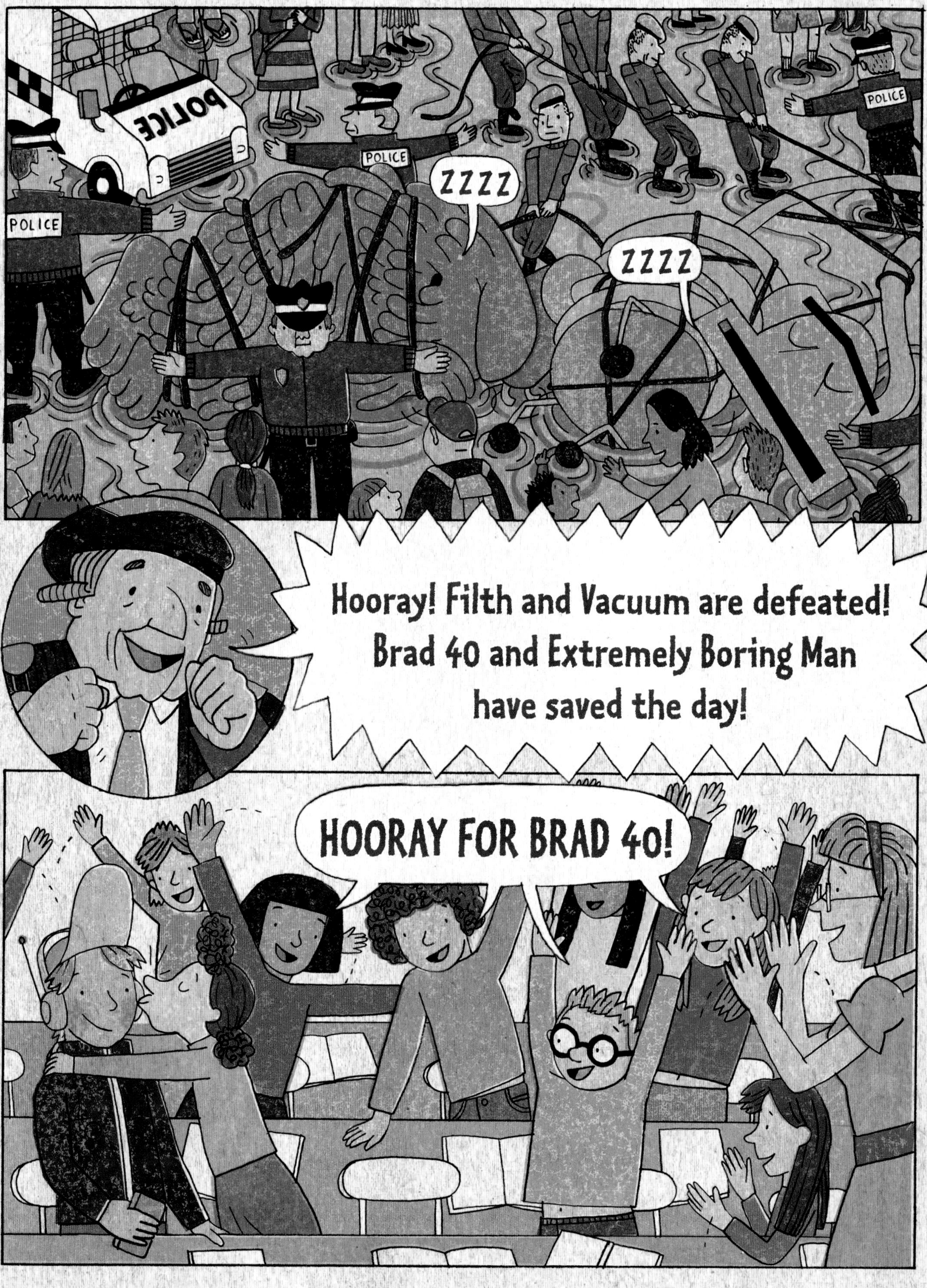
POLICE
POLICE
POLICE
POLICE
ZZZZ
ZZZZ
Hooray! Filth and Vacuum are defeated! Brad 40 and Extremely Boring Man have saved the day!
HOORAY FOR BRAD 40!

"And that," said Dad, "was how clever Brad 40 and Extremely Boring Man saved the world."

Little Elmer and Emily lay in their beds, sleeping soundly.

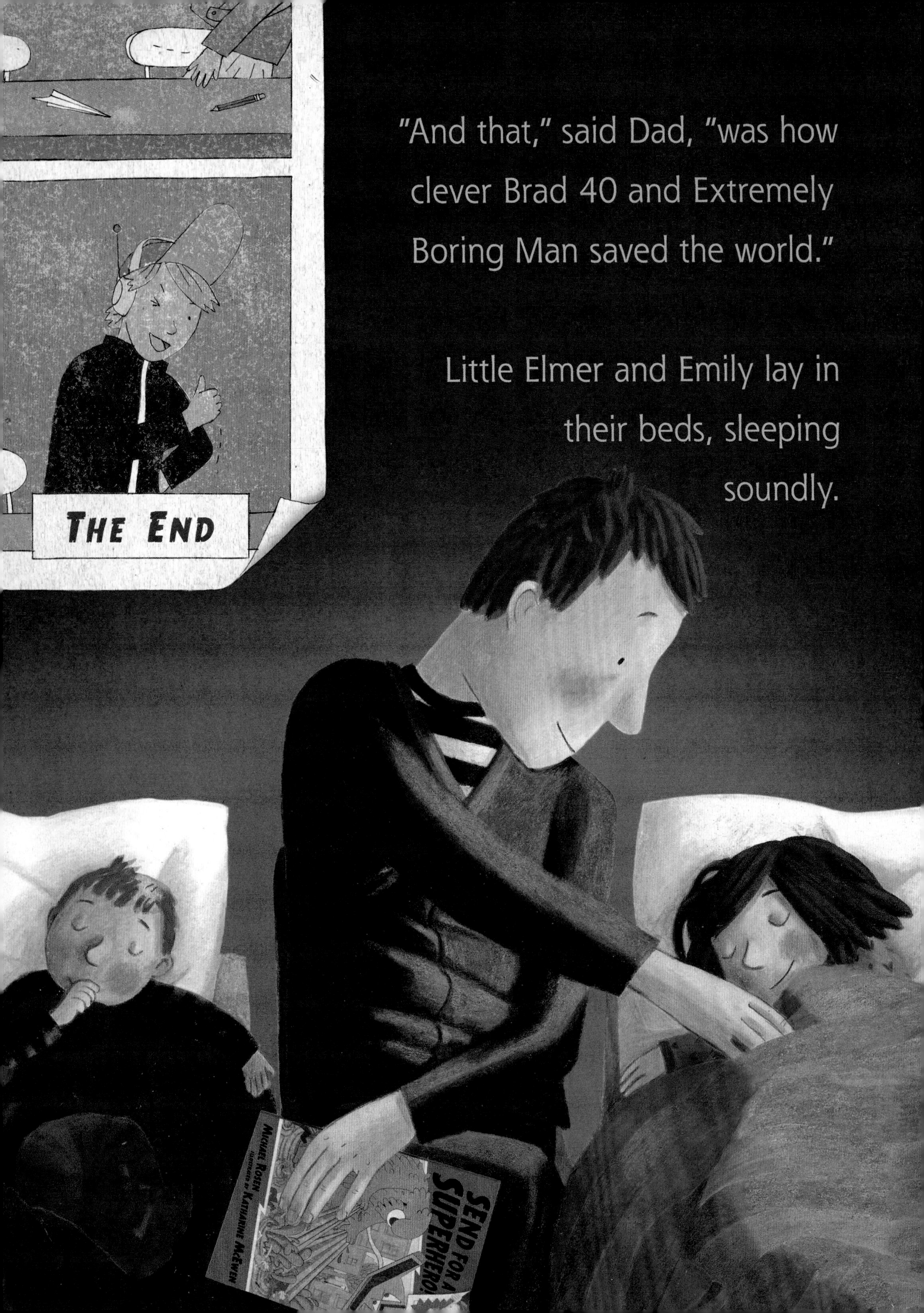
THE END
SEND FOR A SUPERHERO!
MICHAEL ROSEN
ILLUSTRATED BY KATHARINE MCEWEN

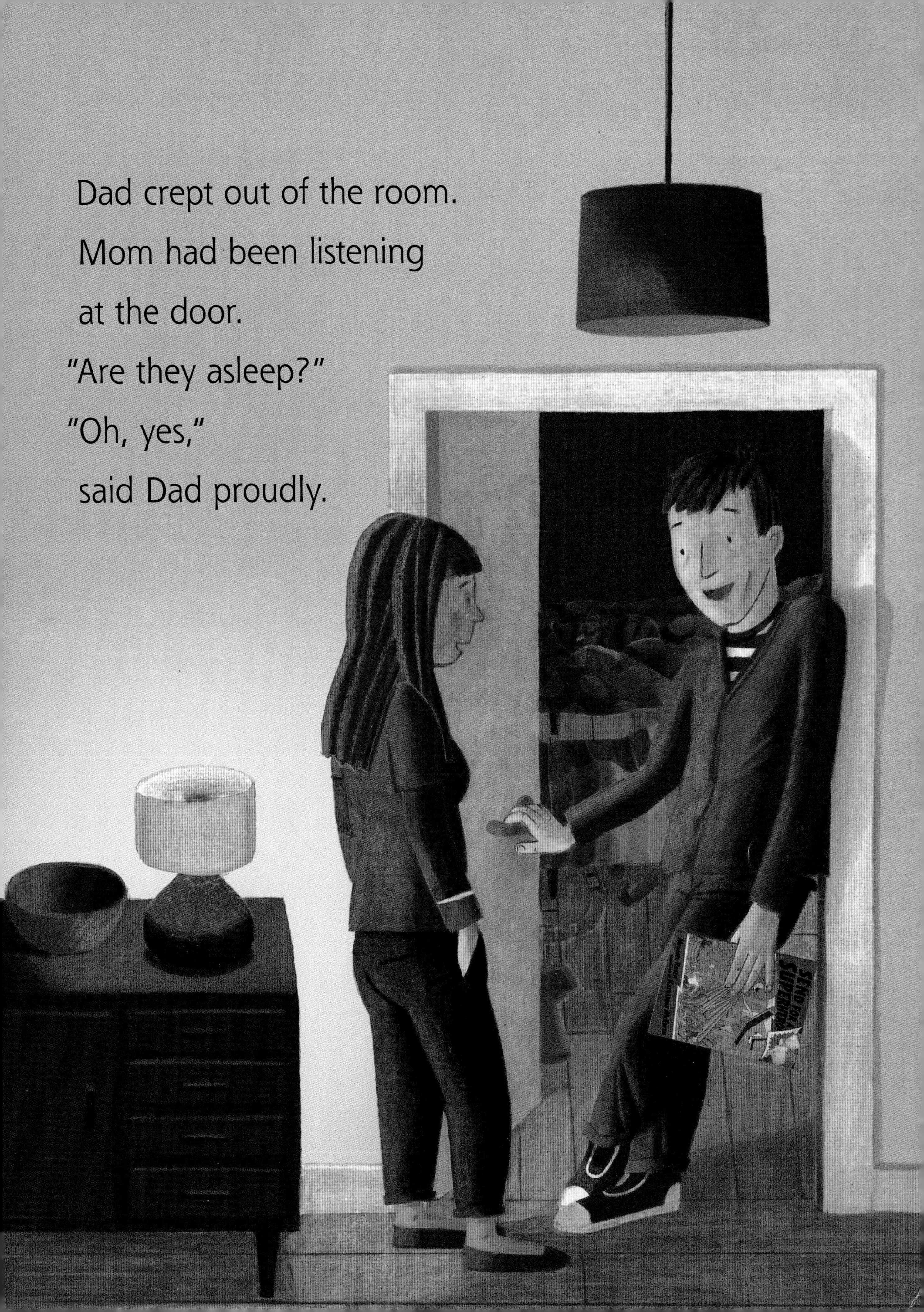

Dad crept out of the room.
Mom had been listening
at the door.
"Are they asleep?"
"Oh, yes,"
said Dad proudly.

"OH, NO, WE'RE NOT!" shouted Emily and little Elmer from the bedroom.

"WE TRICKED YOU!"

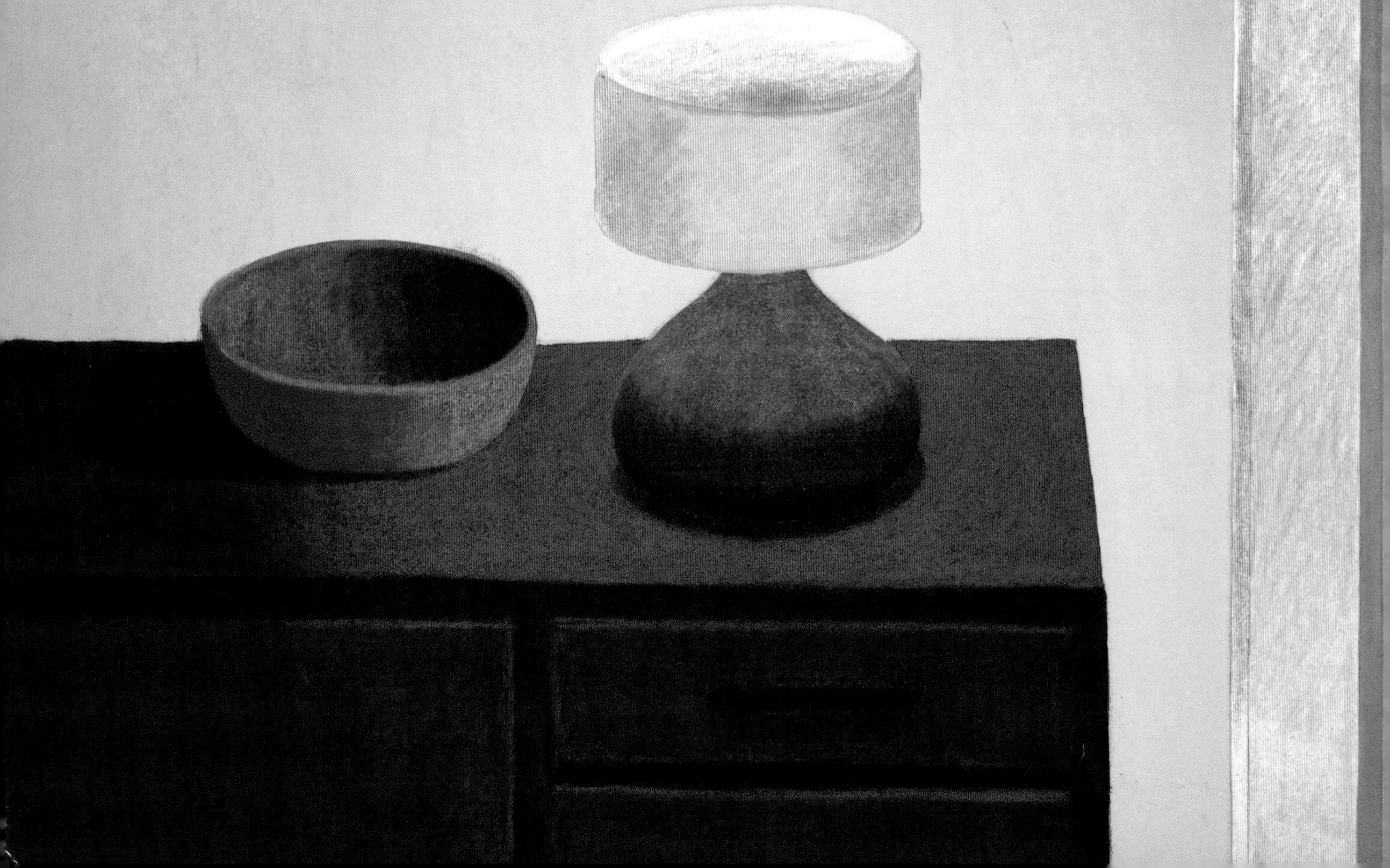

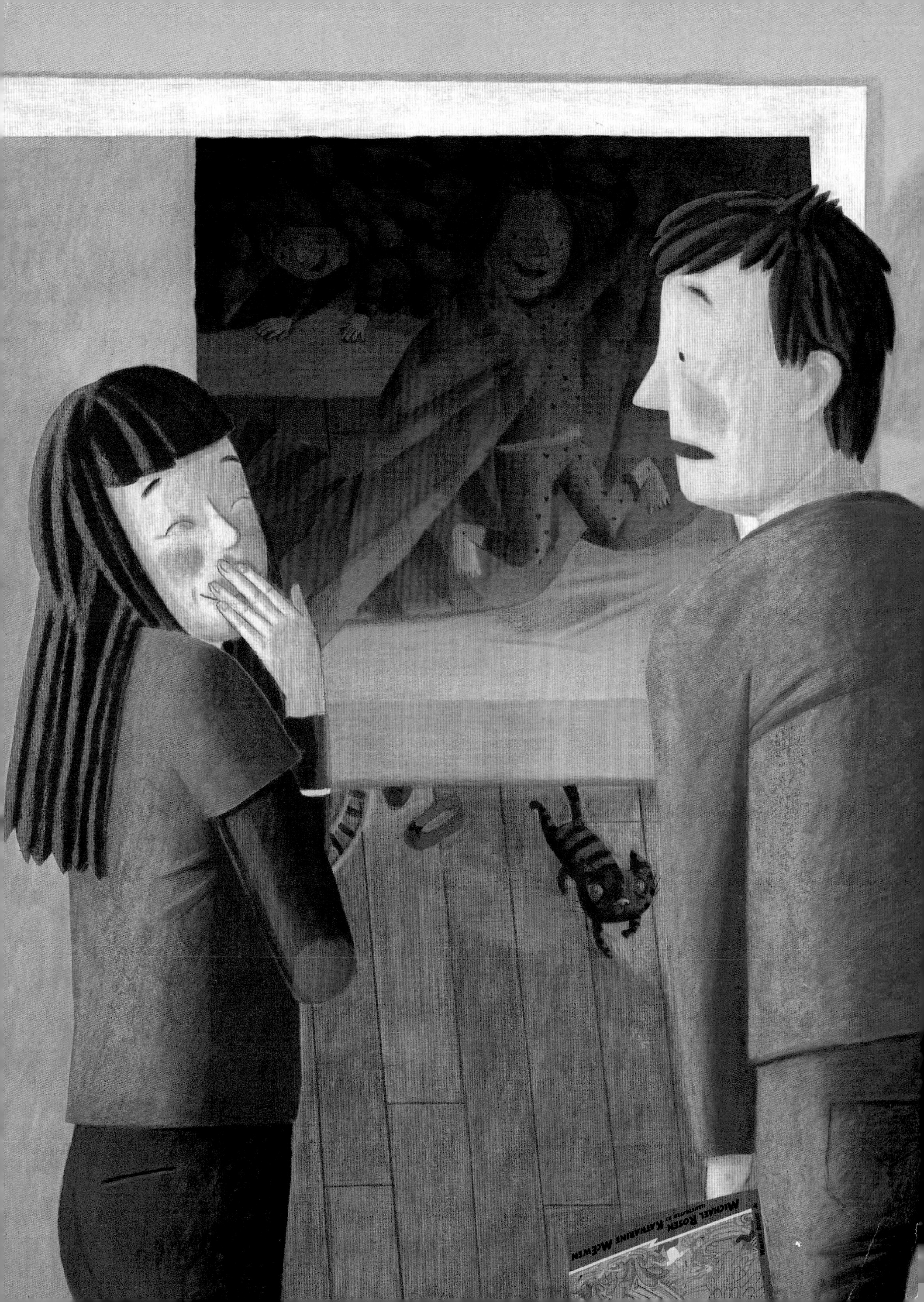
MICHAEL ROSEN
KATHARINE McEWEN

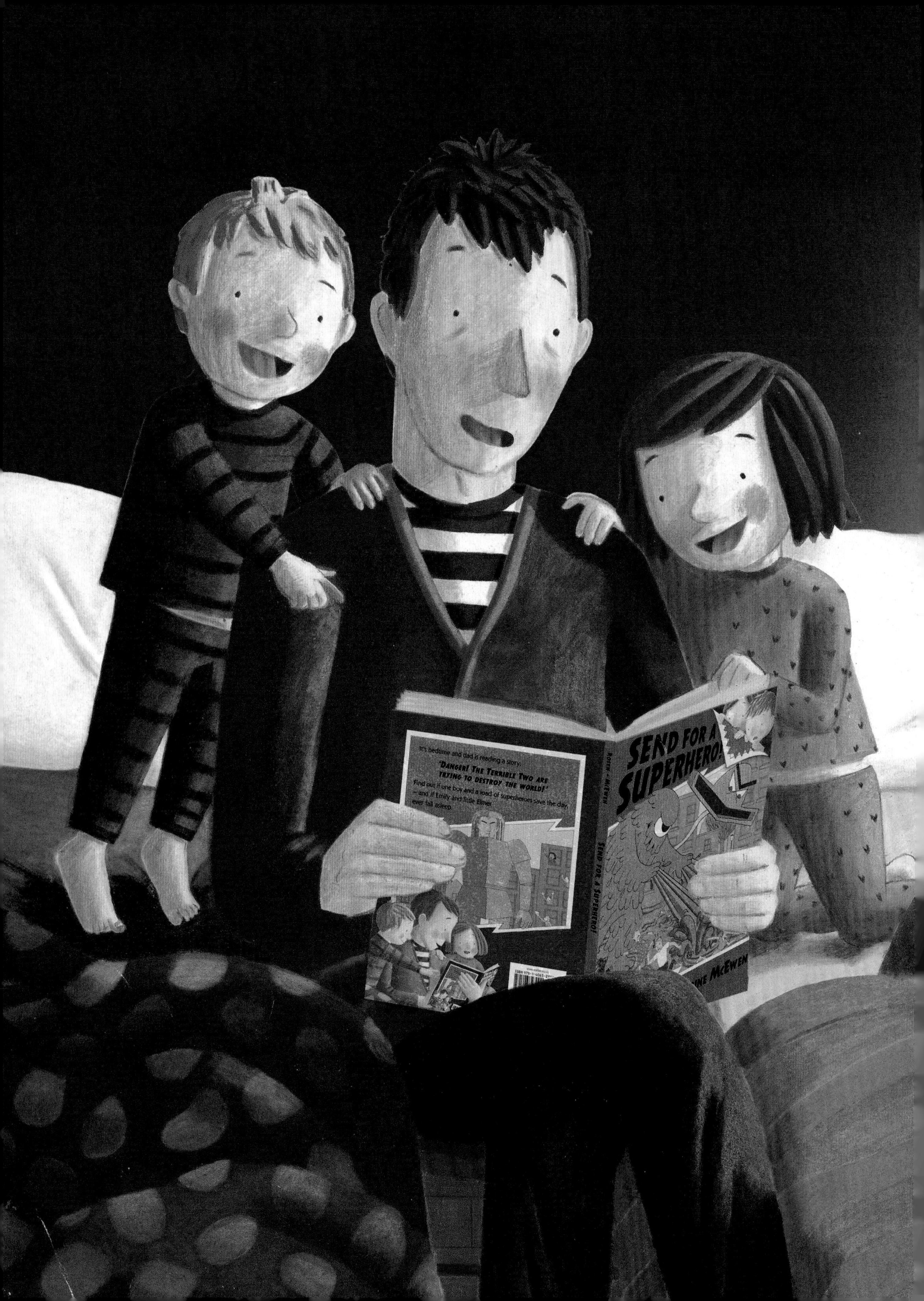
It's bedtime and dad is reading a story:
'Danger! The Terrible Two are trying to destroy the world!'
Find out if one boy and a load of superheroes save the day, – and if Emily and little Elmer ever fall asleep.
Rosen · McEwen
Send for a Superhero!
Send for a Superhero!

And so Dad started on a new chapter
of how Brad 40 saved the world.
Again.

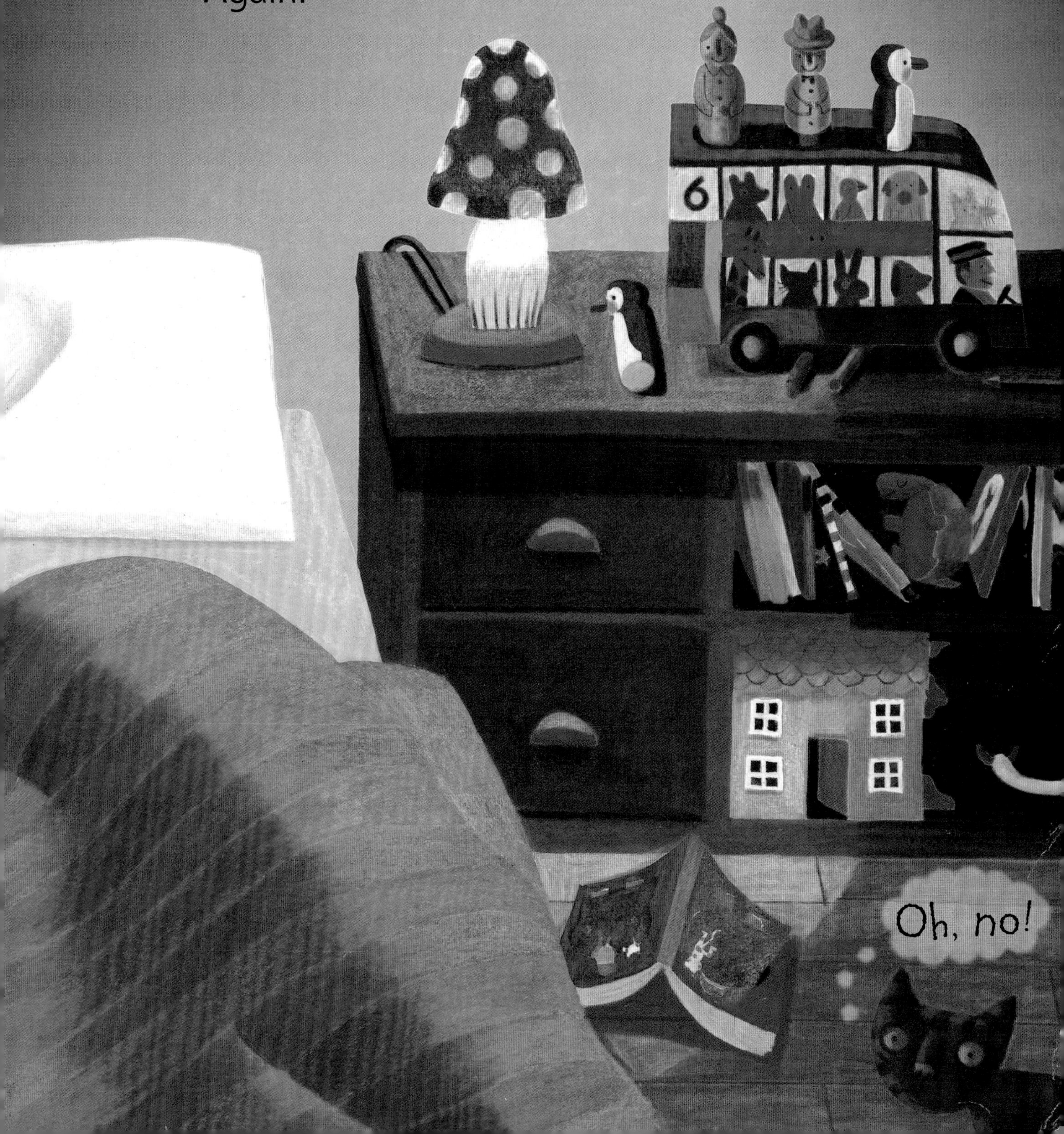
6
Oh, no!